CU00901046

01068

This book is due for return on/before the last date shown below

25/1/02		
18/2/02		
17/12/03		

First published in Great Britain in 1998 by Mammoth
an imprint of Reed International Books Limited
Michelin House, 81 Fulham Road, London SW3 6RB

Just Like Me copyright © 1995 Greenleaves Pty Ltd
First published in *Uncovered!* by Paul Jennings, published by Penguin Books
Australia Ltd
Gift copyright © 1998 Susan Gates
You Can't Have Everything copyright © 1998 Sue Welford
The Lonely Fisherman copyright © 1998 Grace Hallworth
The Melted Chocolate Boy copyright © 1998 Julie Bertagna
Out of the MUD copyright © 1998 Lisa Tuttle
The Bird Boy copyright © 1998 Tim Bowler
One Summer with Hannah copyright © 1998 Keith Gray
The Real Song copyright © 1998 Annie Dalton

This volume copyright © 1998 Reed International Books Limited

The moral rights of the author and cover illustrator
have been asserted.

ISBN 0 7497 2954 6

10 9 8 7 6 5 4 3 2 1

A CIP catalogue record for this title
is available from the British Library

Typeset by Avon Dataset Ltd, Bidford on Avon, B50 4JH
Printed in Great Britain by Cox & Wyman Ltd, Reading, Berkshire

This paperback is sold subject to the condition
that it shall not, by way of trade or otherwise,
be lent, resold, hired out, or otherwise circulated
without the publisher's prior consent in any form
or binding or cover other than that in which
it is published and without a similar condition
including this condition being imposed
on the subsequent purchaser.

CONTENTS

Just Like Me

Paul Jennings from

UNCOVERED!

I love you.

Now that's a thing no self-respecting twelve-year-old would say to a girl.

Well, you couldn't really, could you? Not when she was the most beautiful girl in the class. In the school. In the country. In the whole world. In those days I would have said the whole universe.

A skinny, dorky kid like me couldn't have said it to her.

Here I am, a grown man. Twenty-one years old and my stomach still gets the wobbles when I think about Fay.

Maybe it's because I might see her again. In five minutes or so.

See, we buried a time capsule in the wall of the old school. And Mr Wheeler made us promise to come back exactly nine years later. When all the kids would be twenty-one years old. I feel a bit foolish actually. Probably no one else will turn up. They will have forgotten. I'll be the only idiot there. And I've flown all the way out from England.

I turn my car into Brewer Road. Soon I'll be at the school. Everything looks different. Where did all those office blocks come from?

The old park has gone. And the fish and chip shop. And the pond where we used to catch frogs.

Oh, oh, oh. No. It isn't. It can't be. It must be a mistake. Look what they have done. No, no, no.

The school is not there.

There's a dirty big shopping centre. With a car park and thousands of cars. Signposts. Balloons. Loud speakers. Escalators. Security guards.

They have pulled down the school and the trees and

the bike shed. They have pulled down my dreams and built a nightmare.

I park my car and wander in through the huge doors. Jaws, more like it. I ride the escalators to the top of the mall and look down at the fountain far below. There are hundreds of shoppers. People sipping coffee, staring into windows, pushing trolleys, dragging children, carrying parcels.

There is no one digging out a time capsule from a school wall. There is no one from Grade Six at Bentleigh West State School. And even if there was I wouldn't recognise them.

All I have left is memories.

I think back and remember what I wrote when I was twelve. The letter I put in the time capsule. The letter that has gone for ever. That no one will read. The letter I wrote to a girl I will never see again.

Dear Fay,

My mum and dad are moving to England. So it looks like I will never see you again. Not till I'm twenty-one, anyway. And that's ancient. Anyway, that's how old you will be when you get this letter. If you are there. When they dig out the time capsule, I mean.

I will be there for sure.

I feel stupid writing this. But no one will know. If Luke Jeffries knew he would give me heaps. So would his nerdy mates. They pick on me. Just because I've got freckles. I hate them, I hate them, I hate them.

My first day at this school was awful. I knew I would cop it. I'm not like you. See, you are the netball captain. You are good at everything. You get A's for every subject. The teachers always pick you to do jobs. They hold up your work out the front.

You are good-looking. No – scrub that. You are better than that. I'll tell you what I think about you. It will be all right because no one will read this until the time capsule is opened.

You are gorgeous. If I was a cat you would be the cream. If I was a dog you would be the bone. If I was a rock you would be the waterfall running over me.

You are the top and I'm the bottom. I'm not any good at anything. Except drawing. Mum says I'm a good drawer.

Anyway, I'm getting off the track. I want to tell you about my first day at school. There I was standing out the front with nowhere to sit. In the end I had to use Mr Wheeler's chair. He said, 'You can sit there for the present.'

Everyone gawked at me. You were the only one who smiled.

When the bell went I stayed on my seat. Mr Wheeler said, 'What are you waiting for, Ben?'

I said, 'I'm waiting for the present.'

Everyone packed up. They all laughed like mad. Except you. My face was burning, I can tell you that. Talk about embarrassing.

After that my problems just got bigger and bigger. I couldn't get out what I was thinking. When they picked on me I couldn't say a thing.

I would like you to be my friend. But you are popular and I'm not.

You sit at the desk in front of me. Your ponytail hangs down and swishes across my books. It is gold like the tail of an angel's horse. I would like to touch it but of course I never would.

My stomach goes all wobbly when I look at you.

I wanted to give you something. But I didn't have any money. Mum is always broke. 'Make something,' she said. 'It's the thought that counts. If you want to give a present make it yourself.'

Well, it was coming up to Easter so I decided to draw on an Easter egg. Seeing as how I am good at drawing.

I got an egg and put a little hole in each end. Then I blew out all the insides and started painting.

Three weeks. That's how long it took. I sat up every night until Mum went crook and made me put out the light. It was going to be the best egg ever in the history of the world. I painted rabbits. And a gnome with a fishing rod. And a heart with your initials on it. All covered in flowers.

Mum reckoned it was a little ripper. 'Ben,' she said. 'That is beautiful. It is the most lovely Easter egg I have ever seen.'

So I wrapped it up in cotton wool and put it in a box.

Then I start to get scared. What if you didn't like it? What if you showed everyone and they laughed? What if *you* laughed?

Oh geeze. I'm scared, Fay. I'm glad you won't get this till I'm twenty-one.

It turned out worse than I thought.

As soon as I walked in the school gate I was in trouble. Luke Jeffries grabbed the box. 'Look at this,' he yelled. 'Ben has a cute little egg for Fay. I wonder why?'

All the kids gave me heaps. They really rubbished me. 'Give it back,' I whispered. My face was burning like an oven.

Luke Jeffries threw the box on the ground. 'This is an egg,' he said. 'so we will hatch it.' He sat down on the box and clucked like a hen. The egg was smashed to bits.

I turned round and went for it. I just ran and ran and ran. I didn't care about wagging school. I didn't care about anything. Except a present for you.

I ran into the kitchen and grabbed another egg. There was no time to blow it out. There was no time to paint rabbits and gnomes and things. I put on some boiling water to hard-boil an egg. Then I tipped in some dye.

And that's when it happened. I was angry and rushing around. I slipped over with the saucepan in my hands. The water sloshed onto my cheeks. Oh, the pain. Oh, my face was burning. Oh, it hurt. I'm not a sook. But I screamed and screamed and screamed.

I didn't remember anything else till I woke up in hospital.

My face still burned. But I couldn't touch it. I was wearing a mask. Bandages. I looked like a robber. There were little holes for my mouth and eyes and nostrils.

'Your face will be okay,' said Mum. 'But you will have to wear the mask for a long time while it heals.'

'I'm not going to school like this. No way.'

'You have to,' said Mum. 'You have to wear the mask

for six months or your face won't heal properly.'

So I walked in the classroom late. Looking like a burglar. With my mask on.

No one laughed.

Because someone else was just like me.

You.

Not burned. But just sitting there with a mask around your face.

Where did you get it? I don't know. And you kept on wearing it for weeks.

And I have never said thank you. And tomorrow my parents are moving to England. I want you to know that I . . . No, scrub that.

You will get this when they dig up the time capsule. I want you to know that I . . . No, I just can't get it out.

Yours sincerely . . . No, scrub that.

Yours with thanks . . . No, scrub that.

Aw, what the heck . . .

Love,

Ben.

Well, that's what I wrote all those years ago. Something like that anyway. And here I am exactly nine years later. In the shopping centre. The school has gone. There is no Mr Wheeler and his grown-up class here to open the time capsule.

There is just me and a million shoppers. I can't even tell where the school was. It would take half an hour to walk from one end of the centre to another.

My face healed up long ago. I don't even have any scars. I should feel happy but the school has been knocked down. And there is no time capsule with my letter in it. I guess the bulldozers must have uncovered it. Or it could still be buried, deep under the shops and fountains and car parks. Maybe some of the letters inside were sent to the kids. Who knows? No one would have been able to contact me – on the other side of the world.

One of the other kids might be here in the shopping centre. Maybe, like me, they have come because they didn't know the school was knocked down. But I would never recognise them. Not after all these years. Not now we are grown.

I make my way sadly through the happy shoppers. I don't notice the shouting and jostling and laughing. I reach the door.

And for a moment my heart misses a beat.

For standing there I see something that takes me back in time. Silently standing by the door is a person wearing a burns bandage on her face. Children are staring at her. They shouldn't do that. Neither should I. But my heart is beating fast and I don't know what I am doing.

The woman's eyes meet mine and slowly she starts to take off the bandage. The children gasp. And so do I as her hair falls down behind her like the golden tail of an angel's horse.

Just for a moment I am twelve again. I catch my breath. My stomach wobbles.

I stare at the woman in front of me.

I now that my life is going to be happy. Because she is smiling the biggest smile.

Just like me.

Gift

Susan Gates

I'm standing at the turn-off with Gift Mlungu. We're waiting for the bus to his village. It's a long way away, up country.

Gift is our school's champion sprinter. When he runs in his shorts and PE vest, it makes me trembly inside. He's got speed like a leopard, grace like a gazelle.

My friend Gracie Kainja said, 'Eeeee, he is one sweet guy!'

His nickname is *gudji-gudji* – after a spider that runs like lightning. It's got a body flat as a penny and long racehorse legs. But I don't call him *gudji-gudji*. I call him Gift.

He's tall and slender and proud – like a Zulu even though that's not his tribe. He's seventeen, two years older than me. And I didn't think he even noticed me.

Until two weeks ago, that is, when he said, 'How about spending some days at my house, in the holidays?'

I couldn't believe it! 'Are you sure?' I asked him. 'You want *me* to come to *your* house?'

'I have just said so,' he told me.

So I asked Mum and she said yes.

So here we are, Gift and me, waiting for the bus. There are children watching us from the doorways of huts, from under the mango trees. Some are peeping at us between high elephant grass.

I'm an *azungu* – a white person. I'm the only white pupil at St Martin's school. My mum and dad are teachers here, in Africa. So I go to St Martin's, where they teach. It's a boarding school because most kids come from faraway villages. Too far to go home, except in the holidays. And I don't sleep in Mum and Dad's house. I sleep in the school dormitory with all my friends.

Most times I forget I'm white. When I comb my hair in the dormitory mirror, I think, 'Hey, how did that *azungu* get in here?'

As we wait at the bus stop, I ask Gift, 'Are those children staring at me because I'm an *azungu*?'

Gift laughs. 'No, they are staring at me, because I am so beautiful, in my best clothes!'

Gift's not in school uniform today. He's got a blue denim shirt on and brilliant white jeans. I'm in love. Gracie, my friend, once said to me, 'I tell you, girl, I have got the hots for that guy! He is the handsomest guy in this school!'

She's right. I've got the hots for him too. I'm standing beside him with a great big grin on my face. That's because it's only just hit me. Gift picked me. Me! Over all the beautiful girls in our school. Take Gracie for instance; she looks fantastic dressed up in her red and blue *zambia* with beads plaited into her hair. She looks so tall and elegant.

But he didn't choose Gracie. He chose me. Every time I think about that I think, Wow! And it feels like meltdown inside my heart.

There's an orange dust cloud creeping towards us up the road. 'Here's the bus!' I tell Gift. I'm really excited.

There are loads of bicycles strapped on the roof. It's going to be crowded! Inside I have to fight my way through baskets of dried fish and green bananas and squawking chickens to find a seat. It's so crowded I can't sit with Gift. I'm next to an old mama, eating sugar cane. She breaks off a piece for me.

'Try! Try!' she says to me, in English.

So I say, in her language, '*Moni, Mama, muli bwanji!*' Which means, How are you?

13

'*Eeeee!*' she shrieks in surprise. 'You are white, but you speak like an African.'

I really like it when she says that.

Most of the time I look out at the tea fields. But I keep taking sneaky glances at Gift. I can see him laughing with people at the front of the bus. He's so good-looking, I'm so proud to be with him. I wish he'd glance at me just once. I keep saying inside my head, Look at me Gift, just look at me, as if my mind can speak to his mind. When he looks I'm going to give him my best smile. But he doesn't look – it doesn't matter. He's invited me to his house, to meet his parents. That means I'm his special girl.

While we were waiting at the bus stop I said to Gift, 'Do you have many brothers and sisters?'

It's funny, I don't know much about him, even though I'm his special girl.

'Oh, many!' laughed Gift. 'Many little sisters and brothers! I cannot count them! You will trip over them. They will drive you crazy!'

Gift's mother is waiting for us when we get off the bus. She's shy and doesn't speak English. She has a baby boy on her back.

'*Muli bwanje?*' I ask her. I give her my best smile. I

smile and smile until my jaw aches. I want to make a good impression. I really want Gift's family to like me.

The baby has a string of blue glass beads round his neck. He's eating a passion fruit. The pink juice is dribbling down his chin. I grin at the baby.

'Is this your brother?' I ask Gift.

'Ya, this one's name is Bernard,' says Gift.

The baby peeps over his mother's shoulder. He notices me for the first time. I flash him an extra big smile. He screams! He screams blue murder, as if I'm a monster or something. He buries his face in his mother's dress.

I'm really, really upset. 'Gift, what's wrong with him?'

Gift laughs, 'Oh, don't worry. He has never seen an *azungu*. Not many *azungus* come this far north. He is frightened of you, that's all.'

But I'm still upset. I feel like running away and hiding. I don't like scaring babies. And I don't like being singled out as an *azungu*. Like I said before, until I look in the dormitory mirror, I forget that I'm different.

But Gift just shrugs and laughs. And when he laughs everything is wonderful. His face is like sunshine. And I think, It will be OK. The baby will get used to me.

I'm longing to be on my own with Gift. I'm really impatient, I can't wait. I mean, that's what he brought me here for, isn't it? So we can be alone together? But his family are always around. His little sisters are always in the way. I'm sharing a bedroom with three of them.

When it's bedtime, they don't go to sleep. They sit in a row on their iron cot, just staring at me with big round eyes.

'Where's Gift?' I ask them. 'I want to see Gift.' I haven't seen him since teatime. But they just giggle.

I've got my own bed. But it's embarrassing getting undressed. They stare and stare, like I'm a freak show or something. I try to get undressed under my nightshirt. I pull off my white pants.

'*Aiee!*' cries the littlest one and runs out the door. She's screaming something in her own language but I don't know it well enough to understand what she's saying.

The two other sisters go crazy. They fall about on the bed. They shake with laughter.

'What's wrong with her?' I ask them.

'*Cha*, she is so stupid,' says the biggest one. 'She does not understand. She thinks you are taking off your white skin, like a snake! She thinks you are taking off your white skin and you will just be a skeleton underneath!'

And they both laugh themselves silly.

But I'm not laughing. I'm angry and upset. I don't

understand. I don't want to scare anyone. I just want to belong. I wish Gift was here. I feel lonely, even a bit weepy. And I'm thinking, I shouldn't have come here. It was a big mistake.

I can't sleep. The little sisters are asleep, all in a heap like a nest of puppies. But I'm awake, staring at the ceiling, thinking about Gift. There are two geckos running round up there – girlfriend and boyfriend. They're batting their eyelids at each other. They're transparent and inside their bodies, you can see their little beating hearts.

In the morning, things look a lot better. I tell myself, You were tired last night. From that long, hot bus trip.

The baby doesn't howl when he sees me. The littlest sister doesn't run away. We have maize porridge for breakfast. Gift's mother is really nice. And Gift is smiling that drop-dead gorgeous smile that makes me weak at the knees. I'm really glad I came.

'I will show you my village,' says Gift.

Great! *At last* I'm spending some time with him. On my own. We were never alone at school. Not once. There were always other kids around. And anyway, I only saw him during the day. At night boys can't visit the girls' dormitories. That's a very strict rule at St Martin's.

Gift's village is just the same as lots of other villages.

There's nothing much to see. Just one street with some Indian shops.

But I don't care. Because I'm walking with Gift. Me and him together. I'm so in love I'm dizzy. It's like I'm floating – like walking on bubbles, not on the hard, dusty ground.

Gift shows me a field with yellow dried-up grass, 'That is our football field,' he says.

We buy a can of Fanta and share it. The Fanta's sickly and warm but I don't care.

He shows me a white hut with a tin roof. 'That is where I went to primary school. Mr Austin Jawali was our teacher.'

And I'm thinking, When is he going to kiss me? If he doesn't do it soon, I'll have to kiss him first.

And I'm just daring myself to do it when Gift says, 'I want to introduce you to someone.'

He goes into an Indian shop. I follow him inside. When my eyes get used to the dark, I see that the shop sells saris. There's lots of cloth on the shelves. Some of it is gold and silver, for wedding saris.

Gift says to someone, 'Here is our English guest from St Martin's. Her mother and father are teachers there.'

I wonder why he says 'our English guest' instead of 'my girlfriend'. But I'm too busy looking for who he's talking to. Then I see her – the Indian lady behind the counter. She's eating slices of fried cassava, dipping them in salt. She smiles at me. Beside her is a girl in a blue sari. She's about my age. She's got big gentle eyes, like a deer. She's got gold bangles all the way up her arms. And she's very, very beautiful.

Gift turns to me. 'This is Sunni,' he says. 'My future bride. And this is her mother.'

I forget to be polite. I can't say a thing. Words would choke me.

My brain's racing fast as a *gudji-gudji*. I don't understand. I *won't* understand!

'Go, go,' says Sunni's mother, shooing us into the back room like chickens. 'Go, Sunni. You may help Gift entertain his English guest. Give her tea. After all, it is quite proper. You will not be alone together. The English guest will be your chaperone.'

And now it's like I'm in a trance. It's dark in the back room. Sunni and Gift sit me down on this pink plastic settee. There's a fan going round, *clunk, clunk, clunk* in the ceiling.

Gift says, 'We will not be long.'

And he and Sunni disappear into another room.

Even then I'm trying to deny it.

But there's an oil lamp alight in the other room. And for a minute I see them, like big shadow puppets on the wall. I see her lifting her shadow face up to him. I see the two shadows kiss, so gently and tenderly.

And I can't deny it any more.

I sit waiting and waiting. It's hot. My dress is sticking to the plastic settee. But I'm frozen inside with misery. And all the time, over my head, the fan is going *clunk, clunk, clunk*, in the ceiling . . .

So that's it then. I finally understand. For the rest of my stay at Gift's we all go out together, Sunni and Gift and me, every day, in a threesome. Everyone is very nice. But Sunni and Gift share a can of Fanta. They whisper together. They giggle. They snatch kisses. They're desperate to be alone. So I walk a long way behind them. The English guest – a perfect chaperone.

They're in love. They're crazy about each other. Anyone can see that. I don't blame Gift. I was a fool, I didn't understand. Didn't want to understand. But that doesn't stop my heart from breaking. He was one sweet guy.

Thank God I didn't kiss him. I would have felt an

even bigger fool. But I didn't. And, of course, I'll never do it now.

When I get back to St Martin's I say to Gracie, 'I didn't know Gift was going to be married.'

'Oh yes,' said Gracie. 'When he is eighteen. Did you meet her? She is Muslim, like Gift. They have been promised to each other for a long, long time. Ever since they were children. It is a family arrangement. Did you not know? Your mother knows. Everybody knows.'

So why did nobody tell *me*?

But it's my own fault. I didn't understand. I thought I understood Africa. But I've got such a lot to learn.

I still wonder why Gift asked me to his village. Was it just to be a chaperone? So Sunni and he could spend time together without her mother kicking up a fuss? Or did he like me, just a bit? Still, it doesn't matter now. He loves Sunni, and not me and I mustn't dream about him any more.

I'll get over Gift. Course I will. There are other boys I like. One asked me to dance at the school dance last Saturday.

But you ought to see him running. When he comes powering home, burning up the track, my heart still goes, *ping!* I can't help it.

And now and again, I feel a bit weepy. Especially when I see two geckos on the dormitory wall, girlfriend and boyfriend, with their little hearts beating like mad.

You Can't Have Have Everything

Sue Welford

'Fetch me this, get me that. Clean my shoes. Bring me a flagon of ale, polish this, polish that. That's all you get around here.' Simon sat in the castle kitchen, moaning.

'You want to be in my shoes.' Cin was blackleading the range. Her cornsilk hair was tied up in a scarf. She had a smudge of black on her sweet, pointed nose and her slender arms were filthy up to the elbows. 'At least you're not stuck by this rotten stove day in, day out.'

She wiped her forehead with the back of her hand.

Simon gazed at her. As usual his pulse began to race. He always felt strange when he looked at her, strange and wobbly and weak. She was so beautiful it took away his breath. Even with a black nose and dirt-streaked brow. His dream was to take her away from all this. Sit her up on a white horse and whisk her off somewhere . . . anywhere.

Fat chance. They were good friends, best friends, but she had her sights set higher than a kitchen boy.

He watched as she sat back on her heels. She picked up the white kitten sitting by her feet and stroked it absent-mindedly.

'I ache everywhere,' she said. She held out her hands. Long, slender, lovely, even with the nails cracked and broken. 'Who ever is going to want me looking like this?'

A tear crept out from under her eyelid. It made a grey groove down the grime of her cheek. She wiped it away impatiently. 'Oh, Simon, am I ever going to get out of here?' She sighed a deep sigh of unhappiness. 'I wish my mum was still alive. She'd never have let me become a flipping kitchen maid.' She held the kitten up to her face and wept into its fur.

'Oh, Cin . . .' Simon felt close to tears himself.

Suddenly the door was flung open and a hurricane burst through. One of the stepsisters. The one with the flea-bitten wig and the wart on the end of her nose. She was waving a piece of paper.

'Look, you guys. The king's holding a ball and guess who's *not* going.' She smirked and rippled the invitation under Cin's nose. 'Get my best gown from the attic, you. The purple and black one sewn with precious rubies and pearls. Get rid of the moths and mice and hang it outside to air.'

'Do it yourself,' Cin sniffed.

Cin put the kitten down. It scampered over to the stepsister and began to play with the frayed hem of her gown. She kicked it away impatiently. Then she bent and put her warty face close to Cin's. Her mud-coloured eyes glittered.

'Do it *now*, Worm, or I'll tell dear Ma-Ma and you won't even get to wave us off to the ball let alone have the honour of helping us dress.'

'As if I care,' Cin said.

Simon knew the argument was hopeless. The stepsisters always won. Always. Cin's dad was so besotted with their mother it just wasn't true. Everyone said the marriage wouldn't last.

25

Well, it had lasted so far and everyone in the castle except the warty sisters and the woman herself were worse off.

It almost broke Simon's heart to know Cin was having to help the sisters get ready. He could hear them shouting orders at her even from where he sat in the kitchen polishing the brass.

'Get this, Toad!'

'Do this, Worm!'

The sound of a slap. 'You clumsy twit, now you've smudged my mascara.'

One of Simon's tears fell into the Brasso. Poor Cin, poor beautiful Cin.

Word had come that the king's eldest son was to be at the ball. The handsomest prince in the world it was rumoured. And he was looking for a wife.

Cin sighed when she heard.

'If only I could go,' she said. 'Just one look at him would cheer me up no end. And who knows . . . he might . . .'

'Come off it,' Warty One said. 'He'd never notice you.' She linked her arm through her sister's. 'It's us he'll fancy. We're really cool.' She dug around in her wig and cracked an unsuspecting louse expertly between her fingernails.

On the night of the ball, Simon and Cin leaned over the turret to watch them go. Dad, in his gold frock coat, black stockings and silver-buckled shoes, looked like a star. His wife, bony as a butcher's scrapheap, was stunning in lime green edged with black fur. The stepsisters' dresses were so wide, so full, so heavy they could hardly clamber up the carriage steps. They waved cheerfully as they set off at a brisk trot and disappeared into the snowy night.

'Have fun,' Cin said bitterly. 'I hope you get food poisoning.'

As she turned away Simon could see she was crying, shivering with cold. All *she* had to wear on a freezing night like this was a thin, ragged dress.

He took off his jacket and put it round her shoulders. He did the buttons up beneath her chin. 'Never mind, Cin.' He rubbed his hands up and down her arms to get the circulation going. 'You've still got me.'

She looked at him through the starlight of her tears. 'Yes,' she said. 'That's the problem. I've only got you.'

Charming, he thought, but didn't say it.

As they went down the winding, turret stair she suddenly smiled and linked her arm through his. 'Sorry, Simon, I didn't mean it. It's just that if I'm ever going to get away from this dump it's a prince I need, not a boot boy.'

Simon sighed too. It was no good. She'd never think of him as more than a friend. He'd just have to put her out of his heart. It wasn't fair. It just wasn't fair.

Cin's chamber was in the depths of the castle next to the servants' privy. Outside the door she suddenly leaned forward and kissed him.

'Thanks, Si,' she said.

His fingers lingered on the place where her soft lips had touched his cheek. 'What for?'

She shrugged. 'Just for being here.' She suddenly clasped him in her arms and began to whirl him round, humming the latest dance tune. 'I wonder what he'll look like,' she said tossing her hair free of its scarf. 'I bet he's big, blond and beautiful.' Her voice became dreamy and far away.

'Or tall, dark and handsome,' Simon said, dizzy from being whirled round like a spinning top. He felt dizzy, too, from the nearness of her. She was like a dream in his arms.

She stopped. 'I wouldn't care which. Just so long as he was good-looking and rich and held me like you're doing now.'

'Wouldn't you want him to be nice?' Simon asked.

'Nice?' She looked puzzled.

'Yes . . . you know, kind and gentle and . . . nice.'

'What?' she said. 'Like you?'

He laughed. 'No, not like me. I'm just a poor old boot boy.'

She stared at him for a minute, the frown still on her face. 'No . . . well,' she said. 'You can't have everything, can you?'

She picked up the kitten, turned and went into her chamber without saying another word.

Simon stood there looking at the closed door for a minute. Then he turned wearily and began to make his way up the echoing stairs to the place where his truckle bed was. His heart was heavy. They were stuck there for good. Riding off into the sunset on a white charger . . .? He snorted.

'I wish,' he said out loud.

'You wish what?' The voice came from the top of the stairs.

'Huh?' Simon blinked, dazzled by a sudden bright light. When his vision cleared he saw her. A fairy-godmother. What on earth was *she* doing here? They had been banned ever since one at Snow White's christening turned out to be a witch in disguise.

She waited until he got to the top.

'Well . . .?' She waved her wand in his face. 'Come on, I haven't got all night.'

'It's Cin,' he gulped when he'd got over the shock of seeing her there. 'I want to take her away from this dump that's all.'

'Right . . .' The fairy-godmother closed her eyes and began mumbling.

Simon suddenly panicked. Even if his wish *did* come true it wouldn't be any good. Cin wouldn't *want* to ride off anywhere with him. All she wanted was a handsome prince.

He put his hand on the fairy-godmother's arm. 'No,' he said, 'Stop!'

She looked startled. 'What's up?'

He explained.

'. . . so you want *her* wish to be granted, not yours?'

'Yes, please.'

The fairy-godmother sighed. 'Oh, very well. Where is she?'

Finding a pumpkin wasn't a problem. Simon knew Cook had one in the fruit store. Catching the rats was something else, though. By the time he'd collared six he felt a physical wreck. He'd fallen flat on his face twice. His uniform was a mess. His chin was grazed. And his nose. He caught a glimpse of himself in the polished copper mirror. Tousled red hair, a plague of freckles on his nose, green eyes squinting at himself, silly, crooked grin. No wonder Cin never looked at him in *that* way. What girl in their right mind would?

When he got back to her bedchamber she had already put on her fairytale frock. Layers upon layers of white silk, silver shoes, long white gloves.

She must have heard his sharp intake of breath, the wild beating of his heart. She twirled.

'How do I look?'

'Wonderful,' he breathed. 'Absolutely wonderful.'

But she was gone already. Swinging away up the stairs to the waiting carriage. Already her dream was coming true. Simon could imagine the scenario. Her turning up. The prince all gooey-eyed. Taking her out onto the moonlit terrace. Vowing undying love. He almost threw up.

'Don't forget . . . midnight!' the fairy-godmother was shouting. But Cin was gone, rattling across the cobblestones, out onto the road. Coach wheels churning a moonlit spray of white as it headed for the King's castle.

Simon sighed and turned away.

'Right,' the fairy-godmother said, rubbing her hands together. 'I'll be off. Toodle-pip.'

Sadly, Simon climbed the stairs once more. He shook the fleas from his straw mattress and lay down, closed his eyes and drifted into a restless, heartbroken sleep.

'I just don't believe it!' Warty Two was throwing a tantrum. Things came flying down the stairs. A corset. A set of heated hair rollers. A mouse-trap. 'Where the hell did she come from?'

Cin sat by the hearth, dreaming.

'And he was so *handsome*,' she told Simon. 'He waltzed me out into the moonlight and told me I was the most beautiful girl in the kingdom.'

'You've told me that four times already.'

Simon hadn't said a lot since Cin almost tipped him out of bed in the early hours to tell him breathlessly all that had happened.

'Did I?' She looked at him. 'Did I tell you I forgot the time and almost stayed past midnight?'

'Yep.' Simon raised his eyes to the ceiling.

'Thank goodness he didn't see my gown turn to these old rags.' She plucked impatiently at her dress. Then she sighed and rubbed her feet. 'Those shoes I wore almost killed me. I took them off halfway through the evening and danced barefoot.' Her eyes shone. 'It was wonderful.'

It was surprising she hadn't got frostbite.

'Are you going to see him again?' Simon asked.

Her face fell. 'How can I? I can't let him see me like this. My hair all greasy, my hands filthy, my nails . . .' She pulled a face and put her hands behind her back. 'Beautiful things are very important to him. He wouldn't even know it was me. No . . . I'll just have to live on my memories for the rest of my life.'

'Seems a bit drastic,' Simon commented.

She gazed at him. 'You don't understand, Simon,' she said. 'It was love at first sight. How can I ever forget?'

She was like that all day. All week. Mooning around. Not getting any of her chores done. She just sat around cuddling her kitten and humming to herself. She hardly even seemed to hear the commotion going on upstairs.

'They're mine . . . give them to me!'

'No, they're mine. Here, let me try them on.' It was Warty One and Two fighting over a pair of dance shoes the prince's footman had brought for them to try on.

Simon ran up to see what was going on. He hid behind a pillar.

'No, there's no one else here,' Stepmother was saying. 'It was my daughters who were the belles of the ball.'

It took Simon a second or two to work out what was going on.

'Look!' Warty Two was holding out her foot. A shoe dangled from her toe. 'They're obviously mine.'

Simon's heart was in his mouth. If he told them, he would lose Cin for ever. She would go away on the prince's white charger . . . off over the hill and he would never see her again.

If he didn't, she would be condemned to live here for ever, nothing but a servant in her own home.

'Go and get her,' the footman commanded when Simon had appeared from behind the pillar and blurted out his story.

'You're joking,' Warty One began. 'She wasn't even there.'

But Simon went and got her anyway.

It was so lonely when Cin had gone Simon felt like dying. The fireplace looked cold, empty, the stove pitted and dull. She'd taken the kitten with her. Its little place by the hearth was empty and cold too. Simon put up with it for a week or two. Then he decided he'd got to go as well. There was no point in sticking around if Cin wasn't there. He would never forget her but maybe there would be *somebody* out there who would want a plain old freckle-nosed boot boy and not a handsome prince.

He packed his things. He could hear the sisters yelling at one another. He smiled sadly to himself. They'd have a lot more to fight about when two of their servants were gone.

Before he left, Simon went down to Cin's chamber. The bed, the straw mattress, the moth-eaten sheets. Her scarf lay crumpled like a puddle of rose petals on the floor. He picked it up, held it to his face. He could smell her. Ashes and tar, woodsmoke, blacklead. He sat down, weeping, lost in a sea of misery and despair.

'Si – for goodness' sake, you *are* here. I've been looking for you everywhere!'

Her voice dragged him back to the surface. She was standing in front of him. Face flushed, eyes red-rimmed.

'Cin!'

She burst into tears. 'Oh, Si, he was horrible. He was vain and selfish. All he did was flex his muscles and admire himself in the mirror. He hated my rags, my rotten fingernails. He loved me in that wonderful frock but he didn't like the *real* me at all.'

Simon tried to speak but nothing came out.

'*And* he smacked the kitten and threw a wobbly when it scratched a hole in his best stockings,' she babbled on. 'Oh, Simon, what shall I do?'

Simon shrugged and tried to control the wild beating of his pulse. 'But he *is* handsome and rich, Cin,' he said. 'And you said yourself . . . you can't have everything.'

'I know,' she sobbed. 'But he's not a bit kind or thoughtful or gentle like . . .'

She stopped crying suddenly, her mouth half open. She was gazing at him as if she was seeing him for the very first time.

'. . . like you,' she whispered.

She had escaped riding one of the prince's white chargers. There was plenty of room in the saddle for them both.

'Where shall we go?' Cin said, her arms tight around his waist.

'I don't know,' Simon said. He kicked the horse into a gallop. 'Somewhere . . . anywhere.'

The Lonely Fisherman

Grace Hallworth

There was once a young fisherman who lived in a cottage by the sea. He had lived in the same village all his life yet no man would fish with him and no woman would marry him. All because of a birthmark that blazed across his face from brow to chin.

'Auld Clootie himself set his mark on the boy. The devil claim him body and soul.' So the story went.

Lonely and friendless the fisherman walked along the shore listening to the waves, when far out at sea they roared as they broke over the reefs. He listened to the waves when close to land they whispered their secrets to the sand. In time he learned the language of the sea. She was his only friend.

One day he saw a woman sitting on a rock combing her long golden hair. She was as naked as a newborn babe. As he drew close he saw a sealskin lying beside her and knew then that she was a selchie, a seal-woman. Quietly he came forward and quickly he got hold of the skin, and no matter how much she begged him to return it, he would not.

'If you want the skin, come home with me for a while,' he said.

Finally she agreed to go with him to his cottage.

When he got home he thought about how lonely he was, and how much he wanted someone to love, and to be loved. He hid the sealskin where she could not find it.

That night as they lay together, she touched the raw red welt on the fisherman's face.

'Who bruised your face so badly?' she asked.

'The devil set me apart from others with his sign,' said the fisherman bitterly. 'Because of this I am an outcast in my own village.'

When the woman heard this she was filled with pity for him and agreed to stay and share his life. Still part of her hoped to find the sealskin and return to the sea one day. But not in the first months, nor in the first years did she find it.

As time passed her feelings for the fisherman changed to an earthly love and they became truly man and wife. Yet often as the fisherman walked along the beach and listened to the waves murmuring to the pebbles on the beach, they seemed to say, 'Send her back to her kingdom and her kin. 'Tis not right to hold her against her will.'

One night he said to her, 'I cannot bear to part with you but I will tell you where I have hidden the sealskin so that you may return to your folk.'

But she said, 'I have no wish to leave you. Let the skin remain in its hiding place.'

And now the fisherman was happier than he had ever been in his whole life. Soon she bore him three children, two boys and a girl.

One day the youngest child, the daughter, was playing in the shed amongst the nets and lines, and as she rummaged she found a wooden box. Inside was a beautiful skin of finest silver-grey feathers. The child ran into the house to show her mother. Immediately the mother saw it she was filled with such a yearning to return to the sea, she could deny it no more. She heard the voices of the selchies singing, calling her back to the deep. And she was torn between her earthly love for her man and her family, and for the sea that surged in her blood.

When the fisherman returned home that evening she told him what had happened and of her deep longing to return to the sea.

'I love you still,' she said to him, 'and to lose you would be like losing another skin grown from our love of these past fifteen years. But I cannot help myself. I must answer the call.'

The fisherman was desolate at losing her but he would not hold her against her will. Before she left she said to him, 'If the time should come when you have need of me, and the children no longer need you then come to the place where we first met. Call me and I will answer your call.'

Then she put on the sealskin and at once was changed into a beautiful seal that slipped into the water and was gone.

One by one as the children became adults they left home until once again the fisherman was alone. Alone in his cottage by the sea with nothing but his memories. He went about his fishing without heart.

One day as he wandered the shore he remembered

his wife's last promise. It was as though the little waves that lapped the shore were whispering words with her soft voice, 'If the time should come when you have need of me and the children no longer need you, then come to the place where we first met. Call me and I will answer your call.'

At once he went to the rock where he first saw her and called to her. Out of the sea came an answering cry and through the waves his seal-wife came to him.

'Come now and join me in our kingdom under the sea,' she said. And reaching out to him she led him down, down into the green depths of the sea. Down to a place where everything was a shimmer of green light. Where green sea grass eddied and flowed, moved by quiet currents under the ocean. Where pearls glinted on white sand.

And they were happy and joyous together.

Timeless and tranquil was their life under the sea and they yearned for no one or nothing. Until, as if in a dream, the fisherman's wife saw the birth of a child to their daughter. For the first time since he left the land the fisherman felt an urge to return.

'I must see our first grandchild,' he said to his wife,

'even if it is to hold the bairn in my arms for a brief moment.'

'Then I will go with you,' said the wife. 'But if we return we lose our immortality for we can no longer re-enter the kingdom under the sea, nor can we live on land.'

'So be it,' said the fisherman.

The two set out together and when they came to the shore they took human form and hand in hand walked to the old cottage by the sea where their daughter now lived. She was overcome with joy for she never thought to see her parents again. She took them to where the child lay in his cradle.

He was a lovely bonny boy who gurgled and laughed when his grandparents picked him up and kissed him, as though he had known them always. When they laid him back in his cradle, each placed the hanselling gift they had brought with them from the very depths of the ocean. A beautiful pearl lay on either side of the child's pillow. Then as dusk came down they bade their daughter a last farewell and left the cottage. Hand in hand they walked back toward the shore.

Next morning the dead bodies of a female seal and a male

seal were found halfway between house and sea, with their flippers entwined.

George McPherson of Glendale on the Isle of Skye told this story to David Campbell of Edinburgh, who in turn told it to me. Now I share it with you. Who will you tell it to?

The Melted Chocolate Boy

Julie Bertagna

Tina clacks hangers along the clothes rail like prayer beads.

'You'll shrivel up and die, you know, if something doesn't happen soon,' she warns the face that stares back at her from one of the boutique's mirrored pillars.

A face that's blank with boredom. Her own.

Anything would do, anything at all, just as long as something happens to crack this mind-freezing monotony.

A murder would be good, thinks Tina, as she catches

Isabel's glare in another of the boutique mirrors and speeds up the hanger-clacking.

Even in this heat wave you've got to look like you're doing something useful every second of the day or Isabel will stick you on mop duty. Or worse, toilet-scrubbing.

Isabel is always a horror, but the heat that swarms in and turns searing amid all the spotlights and mirror walls is bringing out her worst. Now she's spotted something in the shopping precinct that's putting an even nippier face on her than usual.

'If that's possible,' mutters Tina.

She slams a foot against the base of the clothes rail and it screams into the stockroom, the arms and legs of the Lycra stretchies sticking out as if they've been shot.

Eleven o'clock and not a single customer.

Tina yawns and checks her make up in a mirrored pillar.

'Droopy hair,' says Isabel, over her shoulder.

Blobby nose, mouths Tina, as soon as Isabel turns her back.

She scrutinises her reflection, fluffing up the hair that sticks sweatily to the back of her neck.

Lip liner's still in a perfect pout though, and the glimmery face glow that cost half a day's wages was worth it, after all. It makes her sparkle. Tina smiles and the dulled expression scatters. The smile makes her eyes turn glittery in the spotlights, she notes, then gasps as a plume of fire shoots up the mirror.

Reflected fire, from something in the shopping precinct.

Tina hurries to the window and peers through the arms and legs of the window display.

DANGEROUS, HIGHLY FLAMMABLE, says a white plastic bottle on the ground.

That's all she can see because a tiny crowd walls up, shoulder to shoulder. And Tina shivers, as if a chill breeze just cracked the heat.

At first, she can only glimpse bits through gaps in the small crowd.

A hand, cupping a tiny flame.

A sleek black ponytail, shiny as a wet eel.

A bare chest, dark-tanned above mottled green camouflage trousers.

Now the jigsaw bits fit together, become a whole person, as the crowd backs off. And the most gorgeous being Tina has ever seen takes up a Jesus pose.

Tina stands on her toes. There's another tiny flame, and another, made quick as a clap in his bare hands. Then it's as if a bit of blazing sun has fallen into the precinct as the gorgeous being throws the fireballs high into the air, and juggles with them.

Isabel's heels click up behind but Tina doesn't move because she can't take her eyes off the young flame juggler's face, calm as an angel's, in its halo of flame.

Her eyes fill up when he closes his and swallows the fireballs one by one.

Isabel leans over the cash desk and Tina feels all her sharp edges because she's so close: spiked fringe, talon-nails and clicky kitten heels.

'NITS,' breathes Tina, as Isabel glares at the flame juggler's small audience. It's Isabel's motto: Not In This Shop.

'Not in this shop,' announces Isabel, right on cue. 'Phone security. Tell them to get here pronto, there's a fire hazard outside my shop. It's frightening off my customers.'

Except it's NOTS not NITS, thinks Tina, as Isabel raps on the window. He's outside, after all.

As she picks up the phone, Tina pictures the boxes and boxes of stock that have still to be ripped out of their polythene wrappers. Snowflakes of flame are falling in the flame juggler's mouth and eyes, falling in his black silk hair.

He could be an Indian brave with those dark looks and his way with fire.

Tina sighs and presses the button for security.

'Shrivel up and die,' she tells a reflection that's split into a hundred tiny pieces by a sheet of mirror mosaics, as security arrive to put out the fire hazard. 'Might as well now.'

The chemical smell hits before Tina sees that it's him. He stinks of paraffin.

Isabel's clicky heels try to beat the flame juggler to the cash desk.

'Security,' she shouts. 'Where have those numpties gone?'

The gorgeous being smiles. 'I'm not here to set you alight.'

Already have, thinks Tina.

'I came in to apologise. I'm no fire hazard though. I know what I'm doing. Don't try it at home though, children.' He winks at Tina. 'Do you sell fire retardant shirts?' he asks.

Isabel points to the door. 'Out.'

'No, really. That sun's hot. I'm coming out in blisters.'

There's no trace of an exotic accent. Under the tan that's as dark and silky as chocolate there are little bubbles of blisters on his shoulders. Tina thinks of the TV advert with rivers of chocolate bubbles, as she begins to fiddle with the label of a shirt.

'We don't serve men. Not in this shop,' snaps Isabel. 'Now get out or I'll have security remove you. Again.'

The young flame juggler shakes his head and turns to go. He stops a moment and looks back at Isabel, annoyed now.

'Get a life,' he tells her. Which isn't too bad, judges Tina, considering all the things he might have said. 'You too – or you'll end up as rat-faced as she is,' he advises Tina as he leaves. 'What a fate.'

'Buzz security,' orders Isabel. 'And tell them I don't want to see that individual near this shop again.'

Tina lifts the phone.

Replaces it in slow motion.

She takes her shoulder bag from the cupboard under the cash desk and walks out of the door in a smooth, slow motion that feels unreal because she's imagined herself doing it so often.

Only an inky stain on the pavement and the chemical smell of him remain. A faint footprint is just outside of the stain and there's a sliver of rainbow in the paraffin. The footprint steps forwards and then there is nothing.

Standing on a bench, Tina scans the bobbing heads that stream through the shopping precinct, searching for a sleek black ponytail – and glimpses it rounding a corner. She chases it only to see a mottled green trouser leg disappearing up the stairs of a number 39 bus.

When she jumps on the next 39 bus that arrives only minutes later Tina has the limbless, flyaway feeling that she gets on Friday pay-days. It's only as the bus takes the road past the gas-works, out of town and into streets of pink and white bungalows, that she jolts back into herself and realises she doesn't have a clue where she's going.

In a panic Tina scans the streets. She even looks in the bungalow windows as the bus flashes past but of course there's no sign of the flame juggler now. Deflated, she gets off at a small row of shops, because there's no reason to go on. Then walks through streets of identikit houses, wondering what she is doing here.

After a while, the bungalows become a pink and white maze and Tina begins to panic that she'll never find her way out. She walks faster, purposefully, to calm herself.

She remembers walking like this before – the day she walked out of school and all the way into town because she couldn't suffer another second in a sludge-coloured classroom. She'd ended up outside the Mirror Mirror boutique, gazing at its window full of dazzle and glamour.

Scorch marks on the wall of a plain little bungalow finally make Tina stop.

Small, black, cartoon explosions.

They're all up the side of the squat, whitewashed house.

When Tina tiptoes over the pink gravel in the driveway the chemical smell is there.

Round the back, everything is absolutely ordinary. A patchy lawn, a wooden bench that you wouldn't put your weight on and a garden hose looping up the path.

Someone chinks the Venetian blinds on the kitchen window and Tina turns to go. Then yelps as if she's been stung by a bee as the back door opens.

It's definitely him.

He's wearing the mottled camouflage trousers, so it must be.

But from the waist up he seems to be melting. The skin of his face and chest is streaky, running off him like melted chocolate.

'Hi.'

It's not particularly welcoming. He draws a paper towel over his face and a smear of chocolate skin comes right off.

The melted chocolate boy takes a step forward and

the ponytail slides off his shoulder. It scatters down the
back door steps like an over-friendly puppy.

It's make up. All of it.

'Make up,' gasps Tina, though she meant to say 'hi' in
the same flat, unfriendly tone. He doesn't even look
embarrassed. She feels outrage.

He's a fake.

'The girl from the shop,' he says and nods, looks all
around and upwards as if he thinks she's dropped out of
the blue sky.

'Boutique,' Tina corrects him.

'Right,' he says. 'I didn't know you at first, out in
daylight.'

He stares and Tina wonders what on earth he means.
She wishes he'd stop scrubbing at the melted chocolate.

'Well, I'll be going then.'

She meant to say it pleasantly, as if there was no
reason at all why she shouldn't jump on a 39 bus and
follow a complete stranger home, but it comes out curt
and nasty.

'What are you doing here?' he demands as she
walks away, on tiptoe, for some reason. 'You live round
here?'

And Tina suddenly has to struggle against tears. There's

almost no chocolate tan left, is all she can think, as he stares at her then gently pulls her up the back door steps and into the kitchen. She tries to fix her runny panda eyes as he makes coffee.

The melted chocolate boy puts mugs of coffee and a packet of Jaffa cakes on the table. Tina watches him dunk a biscuit in his coffee and eat it in one bite.

'Is it a hobby?' he asks, after his fourth Jaffa cake.

'What?'

'Following customers home.'

Tina stands up. Time to go.

'All that warpaint, that hair. You're a complete fake,' she tells him as she makes for the door.

'Well, yeah.'

He looks puzzled.

'What's it to you? What *is* your problem?'

Tina wishes she'd already left because it's nothing to her at all but the fact is that even under the streaky chocolate he's still the most gorgeous being she's ever seen. Even with his face snapped tight in annoyance he looks like an angel. A streaky, bad-tempered angel. Because of that she hesitates.

'*You* should get yourself a life. A real one, not a fake one.'

'I've got one, thanks,' he says, surprised again. 'This is just a holiday job. Something I always fancied trying. I'm a poor student with a penniless summer to get through.'

'Isn't it a bit dangerous for a holiday job?'

'No worries. I did a course. I've got a certificate.'

He's half-smiling at her now, sitting back munching yet another Jaffa cake as if he has decided he may as well enjoy this strange encounter.

'Now, what *you* do is a lot more dangerous,' he tells her through a mouthful of biscuit. 'I saw you this morning. A face called boredom staring out of a window. Life's too short and you're too young to settle for that, surely. More coffee? You've let that go cold.'

As he leans over the table Tina sees the eagle tattoo on his shoulder curl up like paper in a flame.

Even that's a fake.

'Got to go,' she decides, and leaves.

At the bus stop, Tina looks for her make up bag and realises she's left it on the melted chocolate boy's kitchen table. She tries to check her face in a bit of shiny metal on the litter bin, and wonders how she can brazen it out with Isabel.

'You forgot your war paint.'

Tina jumps.

'You really shouldn't go out like that in daylight,' he grins. 'You might frighten somebody.'

'Pardon?'

Tina is about to point out the irony of a streaky mess like him offering make up tips when she realises he's no longer a melted chocolate boy. He's clean and pink-cheeked, a bit sunburnt. Still with the face of an angel though. But a more ordinary sort of angel.

Tina glances in her make up mirror and is appalled by what she sees.

A painted mask.

War paint.

A fake.

And a streaky mess where her tears have been.

The sunlight makes the colours on her face livid, brash. Yet under the boutique spotlights she is glamorous and dazzling. Except she isn't really any of those things. Inside, she's grey and dulled with boredom.

Tina rubs a tissue over her face and chucks it in the litter bin. She feels like throwing in her little bag of make up when it strikes her that it might, after all, come in handy.

She turns and smiles at the ordinary angel who seems

unsure whether he should stay or leave.

'Tell me,' she says. 'How does a girl learn to juggle fire?'

Out of the MUD

Lisa Tuttle

Jennifer had decided to kill Terek.

She didn't want to do it – the big, powerful warrior was a part of herself, after all – but she saw no alternative. Term had ended, and with it the free access to the Internet which had become such an important part of her life. For the next three months she'd be working as a waitress and living without any means of entering the virtual worlds of cyberspace. She would not be able to stay in touch with her friends, and by the end of the summer they would have moved on to other worlds, other adventures, and most likely forgotten all about her. She would be back in

September, but she knew it would not be the same. She would be someone different then – so would they all. She had made up her mind not to go without saying goodbye. Even if they never met again, she could not disappear without at least trying to let Byron know how much he had come to mean to her.

That night when she logged on she found Byron and the Jade Princess waiting for her in the woodland glade, as she had known they would be. Tears welled up, but her hands were steady on the keyboard as she typed in her descriptions of her alter ego's final encounter with his friends.

Terek staggers into the grove, gasping for breath, twitching and quivering in every muscle. He is wearing only a loincloth and bears none of his usual weapons. Although he carries no visible wound, he is clearly in pain and in serious trouble.

The Jade Princess casts a spell of divining, to determine what ails the mighty warrior, and how she can help him.

Byron rolls up his leather jacket to make a pillow and helps Terek to lie down, covering him with a spare cloak.

The spell reveals that Terek is dying. He has been poisoned, and there is no antidote.

Jade Princess howls in despair and disbelief. < No! I shall *pull you back from the jaws of death! Tell me the name of the one who poisoned you and I will create a counter spell! >*

<Too late. I am dying. My time has come. I wanted to tell you, before I go, how grateful I have been for your friendship. I have never told you how much you mean to me.>

Byron holds one of Terek's hands tightly in his own. <Save your strength, dear friend. I know how you feel. Aren't we blood-brothers, soul mates? How appropriate, then, that we should both be dying. As usual, you have proved yourself braver and stronger than I. I had planned to say nothing, merely disappear.>

(Jade Princess): Excuse me, have I missed something? Did I fall asleep for a minute? Why are you both dying?

(Byron): It's called the end of term.

(Jade Princess): Don't you guys have computers at home?

(Byron): Not everyone is as wealthy as you, your highness. I have a laptop, but no modem, no access at home. My folks aren't interested in being on-line.

Jennifer stared at the screen in shock. She didn't know why, but for some reason it had never occurred to her that her fantasy companions might, in real life, be university students no older or better off than herself. Byron and the Jade Princess continued to 'talk' on screen, the Princess complaining, in her self-centred way, about being left to carry on the quest all by herself throughout the summer, and Byron deflating her self-obsession with mildly witty barbs. Then the Jade Princess said, *sniff* *I'm going to miss you, even if you're not always very nice to me. I love you both, you know.*

(*Byron*): *We could have one final adventure. Possibly the scariest yet.*

Jennifer hadn't finished packing, and her brother was arriving to pick her up early in the morning. She typed, **Too late for Terek.**

(*Byron*): *I mean a different sort of adventure. We could meet on the other side. IRL.*

(*Jade Princess*): *Is that a good idea? Our RL selves are completely different. You'd never recognize me. We might be disappointed. It could be a disaster.*

(*Byron*): *Scared, Princess? How about you, Terek?*

Terek not know meaning of fear.

(*Byron*): *Remind me to buy you a dictionary.*

(*Jade Princess*): *Oh, all right, I'll come, too. I'm not letting you boys have all the fun without poor little me! Where shall we meet? When? And how will we know each other?*

Jennifer spent less time than she usually did on-line that night, but after she'd logged off and packed everything away she was too wound up to sleep. In less than a week she would be meeting the RL – real-life – person who existed behind the persona she knew as Byron. The thought made her heart race and her stomach clench. She didn't even know his real name, but she was in love with him. But what would he think of her when they finally met in the flesh? This might be the most wonderful thing that had ever happened, or a complete disaster.

During her first month at university Jennifer had discovered the existence of MUDs, or Multiple User Domains, and her life in the MUD was soon as important to her as the off-line world of classes and studying – and far more exciting. In RL, as she soon came to call it, she was shy and found it hard to make friends. She would have been lonely and miserable if it wasn't for the people she met on the net. Chatting was all right, but what she really liked was the excitement of exploring a fairytale world where magic really worked. In a reality populated by witches, dragons, elves and other colourful figures, she could be whoever or whatever she wanted.

At first she had been a beautiful witch named Rowan, but she quickly tired of fighting off lusty male admirers. This was not a problem she'd ever encountered in real life, and she'd imagined it might be fun to be the object of male desire, but the experience turned out to be time-consuming and far from pleasant. It became a bore, spending so much time outwitting all the lusty giants, lascivious trolls and seductive princes when she would rather have been pursuing her quest for magical wisdom, so she had retired Rowan and rejoined the game as Terek.

Terek was a huge, powerful, scar-faced fighter, master of sword, axe, lance, and a dozen other forms of armed and unarmed combat. He could not use magic at all, but his physical strength was sometimes of more use than magic, as he had demonstrated when he saved the Jade Princess – a high-ranking sorceress of exotic beauty – from the jaws of a huge serpent. Terek was not at ease around women and never made romantic overtures. When the Jade Princess flirted with Terek, as she often did, Jennifer felt a bit peculiar, and Terek was steadfastly unresponsive, usually pretending not to understand. Although grateful for the help of her magic powers, Terek felt more at ease with Byron, a slightly-built, quick-witted man who suffered from a mysterious, unseen wound which sapped his strength. He lacked Terek's physical prowess, but this was compensated for by magical powers including teleportation and invisibility. Byron could also often charm his way out of trouble (even if his penchant for the ladies sometimes landed him back in it) and had a long-running flirtation with the Jade Princess which never became anything more than that.

Jennifer suspected that the Jade Princess was a little bit jealous of the close bond of friendship which united Byron and Terek. Byron was so much fun, so clever and romantic and desirable . . . but his relationships with women were all the same, all shallow, unlike his friendship with Terek, which was real.

The friendship and their feelings were real, only the characters were imaginary. Which meant that the whole situation was impossible. Jennifer knew that Byron was an imaginary character, just like Terek. So how could she be in love with him? Nevertheless, she was. Jennifer loved Byron. But did the person who was pretending to be Byron love Terek? And how would he react when he learned that 'he' was her?

Just because they'd made up their characters didn't mean that what happened wasn't real. When she was Terek and he was Byron they weren't pretending, they were playing, which was different. Getting to know someone else's fictional self, his self-creation, was an extraordinarily intimate thing. They were sharing their fantasies. They had come to life inside a shared dream.

Lisa Tuttle

And now the dream was over. They had agreed to meet in the real world, as strangers, for the first time. Jennifer knew how unlikely it was, how unrealistic, to imagine that they would fall in love, yet that was exactly what she hoped would happen.

Still not knowing each others' real names or addresses, they had agreed to meet on neutral ground, in London, at a Chinese restaurant. They would know each other by the pink flower pinned to shirt or jacket. Up to the very last moment it was still possible to chicken out, vanish, never to be found by the others.

Jennifer hardly slept all night, got up on time, but then dithered about so nervously that she wound up reaching the station too late for the express train and had to settle for a much slower one. Once she got to London she managed to get lost, so that by the time she reached the restaurant she was at least fifteen minutes later than the time agreed.

Bursting through the door she saw them at once, two scruffy student-types dressed almost identically in baggy, faded jeans and t-shirts, the blossoms glowing like little pink hearts. They looked to be about her own age. One girl, one boy.

The Jade Princess and Byron turned at the opening of the door. She was aware of their eyes checking out the pink flower on her chest, rising to her face, then checking out her chest again. She saw the startled smiles and read their emotions – surprise, relief, pleasure – as if they'd been written on a screen in front of her. Terek was a girl! Terek was a girl, and that was OK.

Time seemed to slow. It took ages to cross the floor. When she reached the table, he took her hand. *Byron*, she thought dizzily. He was so real, so vivid! And yet nothing like the small, dark, saturnine figure from their shared fantasy. The real boy was tall, lanky, fresh-faced, and fair. She struggled to absorb all the details: the speckled blue-grey-green of his eyes, the glinting golds and browns of his thick, short-cut hair, the texture of his smooth cheeks. 'I'm Tim Richardson,' he said, holding her hand.

'Amanda Speck,' said another voice. Jennifer turned to look at the Jade Princess. Of course, she hadn't really thought the real person behind the Princess would be an oriental beauty, but this tall, red-headed, blue-eyed, pale-skinned girl was something of a shock. 'Are you going to tell us your name?'

'Jennifer. Jennifer Allason.'

'Well, sit down, Jennifer, and let's get lunch. Tim, let go her hand, there's a good boy.'

'Sorry.'

Jennifer was sorry, too. It had been nice holding his hand. She saw the pinkness of a blush rise in his cheeks and then their eyes met. She felt a warmth in the pit of her stomach. He liked her!

What followed was surely the most peculiar meeting ever. They were strangers, so conversation for the most part was about the obvious, the ordinary, searching for points of contact: where they came from, what they were studying at which university, what music, books, and films they liked best. They might have been any trio of students meeting by chance for the first time. But always, lurking in the shadows behind them, or hovering overhead like unseen angels, were Terek, Byron and the Jade Princess. Jennifer felt a strange thrill whenever these unseen presences were invoked and details from the adventures they had shared were brought up. She had never talked to anyone about her experiences as Terek, had never even said any of the names out loud before today. They had belonged to the written, not the spoken world; they had belonged, she'd thought, to the world inside her head.

In a sense, this public sharing of what had been a

private experience should have made it seem more real, yet it made her even more aware of how unlike Byron Tim was. She knew she should not have been surprised — how much of Terek did he see in her? — but she felt confused by her inability to find the character she loved in this rather awkward young man seated beside her.

But she did like Tim, she decided. He was nice, even if a bit egotistical and lacking in humour. She kept waiting for Byron's wit to reveal itself. As time slipped away she became more and more certain that he liked her, too. She thought that Amanda was a bit annoyed by how obviously he preferred Jennifer to her, and recalled how the Jade Princess had always liked to be the centre of attention, unhappy when excluded by the closeness between Byron and Terek.

When Amanda excused herself to go to the ladies' room she paused to give Jennifer a look which Jennifer ignored. It wasn't that she disliked Amanda or didn't want to be friends, but just now it was Tim she wanted to get to know better. He took advantage of their time alone, as she had hoped, to suggest they get together later, just the two of them. 'Tell her you've got an early train to catch.'

Soon after Amanda's return, Tim excused himself.

'More tea?' Jennifer asked.

Amanda smiled and gave the tiniest head-shake. 'Maybe later. There's a brilliant patisserie in Soho . . . we could go there afterwards, if you like. I've already told him I have to catch the first train home – you could say the same.'

Jennifer bit her lip to keep from smiling. 'Actually, I've already agreed to do something with Tim.'

'Uh-oh, you didn't think fast enough!'

Amanda's mocking smile reminded her of something, but she couldn't quite put her finger on it. 'What do you mean? I like him,' she said stolidly. 'Really, it's kind of a dream come true. I was so afraid this would be a disaster . . .'

'Me, too.'

'That we wouldn't like each other at all, or, or that he'd like you better. After all, he might have expected me to be another bloke . . .'

'I'm sure he did,' said Amanda. 'You could see how relieved, how *pleased* he was, when you walked in here. Especially after he'd struck out with me.'

That was a sting in the tail she hadn't expected, but of course the other two had been alone together in the restaurant for a quarter of an hour or more before she arrived, and it was in character. At least, it was in Byron's character. She said, bravely, explaining it to herself as much as to Amanda, 'Oh, well, it's not surprising he'd ask you out first, especially since he still thought I was a man, and, after all, as Byron, he was in the habit of flirting with the Jade Princess. How could he resist? I was worried myself that you'd be irresistible; you always seemed so sure of yourself, so super-feminine that every man would have to fall for you . . .' She trailed off, alerted to something wrong by Amanda's expression.

Amanda said, 'Hold on. You thought *I* was the Jade Princess? Oh, no, no. She's not my style.'

Tim was returning; Jennifer glimpsed him from the corner of her eye, but could not look away from Amanda's sharp, lively face. Suddenly that mocking smile was incredibly familiar.

Her heart lurched in dismayed recognition as Amanda said, 'I thought you realized. I'm Byron. *He's* the Jade Princess.'

The Bird Boy

Tim Bowler

He hated lying as he filled out the application form, though he knew there was no alternative. But what he told them at the interview – albeit in the clumsy speech which he could not help yet which he knew others found irritating – was the truth.

The first question he had expected.

'What is it that drew you to apply for this job?'

To which he replied that he just felt the job was right for him and that he had something to offer to it, if they would only give him the chance – adding, after a moment, that he'd dreamt of the location several times and recognised it from the photograph, though he'd never been there.

'You claim in your application to have lots of experience, yet you appear to have no qualifications. Why should we choose you for this post?'

He had no answer to this. But, to his relief, they decided to test him rigorously; and things went much better after that. But the questions kept coming.

'Your specialist knowledge is certainly impressive, but character is also an issue here. How can we be sure that you have the inner resource to withstand long periods of solitary work?'

To which he said that not only did he believe he possessed such inner resource but that he was actually drawn to the solitary life by temperament. There would be no danger of loneliness, and besides, he would not be alone: he would be with the birds – and birds were his friends.

At which point they looked at him strangely for a moment. Then the questions resumed, and went on endlessly, endlessly, until he felt certain that sooner or later someone would prise from him the things he yearned to conceal.

But no one did. In the end, they saw what they thought

they saw: a young man with a large, clumsy body which shuffled in the chair like a caged bird chafing for release; a young man who found it hard to look them straight in the eye, so inarticulate that they had nearly discounted him outright – until he spoke of birds, when suddenly his words caught fire. They saw a young man of independence, with eyes that spoke of much experience; a young man who was somehow an old man; a man who lived a deeper life. And what they saw seemed finally, against all logic, to answer their needs.

They did not ask about the boy because they did not see the boy. So he never needed to tell them that he was not twenty, as he had written on the application form, but sixteen; that his parents had died when he was seven and he had no brothers or sisters or relatives; that he had left his foster home and was never going back; that he had dropped out of school without taking any exams.

That he had three months to live.

Perhaps a little more, perhaps a little less.

'It's hard to be precise about how long,' Doctor Payne had said with her usual bluntness, wrinkling her nose as though she were at quiz night in the pub, trying to remember the date of a battle. 'It's a very unpredictable disease, you see. The only thing that's absolutely certain about it is . . .'

But she had stopped there. There were limits, it seemed, even to Doctor Payne's capacity to offend.

He remembered sitting very still as she rattled on about medication to relieve the pain, and the hospital, and diet, and having a positive attitude, and sundry other things, all now mercifully irrelevant; and he remembered feeling strangely detached, almost light in body and mind, as though a breeze could waft him away. The last thing he recalled was her startled face as he stepped over, stopping her words in mid-flow, and gave her a kiss, before walking out into the soft morning rain.

The island was small, barely a quarter of a mile across, but he loved it at once. The mainland, with its memories of schools and hospitals and foster homes, was pleasantly remote and often obscured by mist so that he felt he was in a strange, limpid world he shared only with the birds. The duties would not have been onerous to him in his stronger days and he resolved that they would not master him now, at least in the beginning.

'The position of warden requires a special kind of person,' ran the pre-interview blurb from the Trust. 'The successful candidate will live on the island and be responsible for overseeing the habitat of the birds on the reserve, counting the bird populations and monitoring their movements, recording the species resident on the island and generally looking after their environment. He or she will also maintain the footpaths and keep them safe and in good order, check water levels where necessary and show visitors round the island. Apart from a first-class knowledge of marine birds and their behaviour patterns, the warden will need to be a person of independence and character. There are no other people on the island. In the summer months there are usually two or three boat-loads of visitors per day, but after September when the majority of the birds have gone, or during bad weather, the number of visits from the mainland will be substantially reduced and there will be many days when there are no visits at all. Persons considering this position must be fully aware of what the job entails. If you do not like your own company and do not possess the required levels of practicality, knowledge and self-reliance, you will not be suited to this post and are unlikely to stay the course.'

But he would stay the course. Solitude was a blessing now. He did his best when visitors came, but it was hard. It had always been hard. Company had never sought him and, as a result, he had long since ceased to seek it in return. He showed visitors round as courteously as he could, answering their questions about razorbills and kittiwakes and guillemots and shags; and they listened to him, because his knowledge was great, and because he was the warden. But even as they listened, he sensed them withdrawing from him. It did not hurt him so much now. After all, he told himself, they had come to see not him, but the birds.

He, too, had come for the birds, and for the ocean solitude. Yet the thought of dying here in this wild seclusion still troubled him. He knew it was the best solution his nature could devise, but he knew, too, that it would not be enough to fulfil his greatest hope.

He had counted on adulthood changing him from the bumbling tongue-tied boy he knew he was to someone who could not just express love but might even one day receive it. And not just any love: he wanted a love he could give his whole being to, one which would return to him, cherish him, make him feel whole, special, wanted. But as life faded, so too did hope.

In place of hope he forced himself to work, hungry for the last vestige of experience, always happiest when the visitors had gone and he could restore his thoughts to the bird life around him. And sometimes, alone with the island and the birds, his mind grew so absorbed that his body lost its claim on him and he found he could work for hours.

But at night, when he sat down in his cottage and ate his food, he felt the tiredness and pain return, each time deeper than the day before; and he began to wonder whether, after all, he truly had the character for this, the final work of his short life on earth.

In his solitude, he did what he had always done: he talked to the birds, about his life, his feelings, his fears.

'I know people don't like me,' he said to them as he walked about the island. 'I don't blame them really. I don't like myself either very much. I'm all closed up inside. I'm not good at saying the right things. Maybe if Mum and Dad had lived longer, they'd have taught me how to talk to people.'

He stopped for a moment and gazed out over the sea.

'But I can't blame Mum and Dad. It's not their fault. Talking to people is just something you can do or you can't. And I can't, simple as that.'

He looked back at the birds squawking round the rocks.

'You're my family now. You're my friends. It's easy to love you. You demand nothing of me.' He frowned suddenly. 'But you don't really care about me either. Why should you? You don't need me in your lives. You've come here to breed and then you'll fly off back to the ocean. And when you return, I'll be long gone.'

He sat down on a rock and stared at the ground, trying to believe there was something still to live for. But his mind saw only despair. He stood up and slowly made his way back to the cottage. And the day closed in like a cloud over the world of his dreams.

It came on a wild morning, with wind and wave lashing the island, and gulls screaming. He had risen early by a strange compulsion and put on his clothes to go out and watch the dawn.

It lay against the door and rolled into the room as he made to go out, a large, strange, very beautiful egg of a type he had never seen before and never could have imagined. The egg was warm and close to hatching, as he could hear a light tapping under the shell when he held it close to his ear; but there was no sign of a parent bird, no clue to its appearance, nothing but mystery.

He took it in and covered it, and kept it warm, sitting with it for many hours, wondering why it was there, and glad that the weather was too bad for visitors. And while he sat, he studied his books, searching for a likeness to the egg, or some description, but there was none; it was unique.

Outside the waves were tipped with iron.

Eight weeks after hatching, the bird was fully grown. The boy had long since ceased to wonder about the strangeness of it. Why, for example, it never seemed to eat, though he had tried many times to feed it, and watched closely to see where it might be finding its food; why it was a species of bird larger than any on the island, yet none of his books had a description of it; or why it never tried to fly, despite powerful wings.

He no longer wondered why the bird never left his side, day or night, or why, when people were on the island, no one seemed to notice it. It was conspicuous enough. It waddled around after him, comical and clumsy, and now enormous, and it was never more than a few yards from him, yet even when he had experienced birders with him, not one of them remarked upon this strange unknown species of bird. On one occasion he had even pointed to it and asked the group what they thought; and one of the party had simply commented on the puffins beyond. Even the other birds seemed not to react to it.

It was strange, too, the almost obsessive way the bird

stayed with him. He had supposed at first that it had taken him to be its mother, since he was the first thing it had seen on breaking out of the egg, yet it kept a distance from him and would always move back if he tried to touch it or offer food. He almost felt as though he were under observation, in the same way as he was observing the other birds on the island.

In the beginning he had asked many questions; but now he asked none. The bird's company gave him a strange joy, and that was all he needed. The outside world drew further from him and the days and nights passed in a twilight of contemplation.

The weeks were passing, too. July was almost gone and he sensed the restlessness in the birds. The sea was calling them back and the air now seemed to resound with the clap and flap of departing wings. He had much to do, recording numbers, movements, changes.

And feeling the changes within himself.

The big bird still followed him everywhere, like a strange watching shadow, and seemed to have no desire of its own to soar away to the ocean skies. At the end of the day, when he went to sleep, there it would be, watching him by the bed; and when he woke in the morning, he would find it in the same place, as though it had not moved an inch. And sometimes, during the night, when the pain woke him, as it did more and more now, in spite of the medication, he would peep out from under the covers in secret and see the dark outline of the bird, its beak shining in the moonlight, its eyes upon him like black stars.

More days rolled by, and more birds left the island, rising in great clouds to cruise out on the racing winds. He stood on the bluff and watched, his strange companion as ever with him.

'Why don't you go with them?' he said to the bird. 'You're an ocean creature, though I don't know what you are. You don't exist according to my books. I've never even seen you try to fly. But I know you can. With wings like yours.'

He stared into the distance at the dark scudding forms.

'There's nothing to keep you here. If I had wings, I'd fly after them. And one day . . .' He frowned. 'One day maybe I will.'

He turned sharply round and the bird moved back.

'It's OK,' he said quickly. 'I didn't mean to startle you.'

But the bird was not startled. It had merely been keeping its usual distance from him. He knelt down and looked at it.

'Why won't you let me touch you? You follow me everywhere and you must know I won't hurt you. But you always move away when I try and stroke you. And why don't you eat? Or fly?'

The bird watched him in its quizzical way. He stared back, trying to pierce the silent speech of its eyes; then he smiled.

'I'm glad you haven't gone with the other birds. I'm glad you're here. You've made me happy. In a funny kind of way.'

He stood up, forcing the pain from his mind, and gazed back towards the horizon and the myriad shadows coursing the sun like darts.

'Maybe there is a paradise after all,' he said.

It was on a Sunday, the last in September, with autumn in the air and most of the birds now gone, that the mist cleared and he saw the launch approaching across a windless sea.

No visitors again – there had been none for several days now – but just supplies and the usual brief, awkward chat with the men. He hid his stick at the foot of the jetty and looked for the bird.

There it was, waddling towards him from one of the

rock pools. He smiled as it walked past him to the end of the jetty as though to greet the men, who – he knew – would not even notice it.

Sure enough, they merely threw the hawsers over the mooring posts and started lumping the stores onto the jetty. They were civil enough but they too kept him at a distance, never having worked out what to make of him. Instead of conversation, they joked among themselves about football and fishing and real ale.

He barely listened. He was watching the bird, standing as if rooted to the end of the jetty, its eyes away from him for the first time and fixed, it seemed, on the horizon. Always, when he had looked for the bird, he had seen its eyes on him – but not now.

It was then that he realized that the bird's time had come.

And, with it, his own.

The men were still talking as they worked, and they even threw the odd question in his direction; but he gave no answer. He was absorbed in the bird, its body still rigid, its eyes unwaveringly turned towards the distant skies.

'Shall we carry the stuff up for you like last time?' the skipper said.

He shook his head, not even glancing at the man.

'And there's nothing else you need? Nothing for us to take back to shore, like?'

He shook his head again. The man cleared his throat.

'Well, we'll be on our way, then. Let's hope the rain keeps off, eh?'

He said nothing, his gaze still fixed on the bird. The man called out something – it sounded like goodbye – then the engine started and he heard the hawsers being slid free of the posts, and the receding sound of the boat as it chugged back towards the land.

When he finally took his eyes from the bird, his whole world had changed. The sea and the sky had become one, and he and the bird and the island had somehow become one with them. The launch had dwindled to a speck; and his eye passed through it like a javelin, effortlessly.

He stooped to pick up his stick.

It took him a while to realize he had collapsed. Gradually his mind noted the sensations: the damp timbers of the jetty beneath him, the smell of salt, the silence like a tomb, and, strangest of all, the powerful warmth flowing through his temples, around his head, beneath his neck.

'Why now?' he murmured to the bird. 'Why touch me now?'

The bird did not stir.

He moved his head painfully to the side and tried to focus his eyes upon it; but all he saw was a haze of blue. He spoke to the bird again.

'Is it time now?'

The warmth seemed somehow to swell more deeply around him, though still the bird did not move. He closed his eyes, feeling as though he were discarnate already.

Yet the scent of the bird, the warmth and softness of its body — those things were of this world, as was the singing of the sea, and the breeze washing over him. He breathed more slowly now, his mind moving in and out of dream-like lands, and he knew little save that his body clung to him no more.

It was only when his call came that he felt the bird stir.

Dimly he heard a distant hum. It was the launch returning; he had lain there a day and a night with the bird. The hum gradually turned to a roar, ringing in his head with great force; but nothing to fear after all. His eyes moved upwards to settle in his brow and, as they did so, he saw the great bird blaze into flight, wheeling away into the ever-circling sky.

One Summer with Hannah

Keith Gray

Matty had a secret. I told him I didn't care, but I think he knew I was lying.

The summer holidays were inevitable now. We may not have believed it back in February but they were so close now we could almost taste them (and they always

tasted something like strawberries to me). One week. Just
one school week was all we had to endure before the
long golden days, cool evening breezes and full six weeks
of freedom were upon us. I knew that by Friday I really
wouldn't care about Matty's secret; by then I'd be in too
much of a rush to get home, get changed and get down
to the park for the first game of football of the holidays.
But today was Monday; I still had five days to go. Five
days of Matty's incessant, irritating, aggravating talk of
secrets. So I had to know. I just had to.

It took me the whole of the morning to get him to
talk. I had to corner him at the end of maths, and even
then he made me guess, giving me clues; it's about a girl,
it's about the summer, it's about a girl *and* the summer. He
loved his game and I hated letting him see my frustration;
it wasn't often Matty had something anybody wanted. But
it was worth the torture in the end. Hannah was coming
back. He'd overheard Becky Flowers and Gabby
McCammon talking about it in registration. Hannah was
coming back for the summer to stay at Becky's house
and the two girls had been planning everything they
could do together during the six weeks holiday. It was
fantastic news, maybe the best news I'd heard all term (if
not ever). I asked Matty if he'd told anybody else and he

assured me he hadn't, but I knew he was lying.

I thought of what it would be like to spend the summer with Hannah. And decided it would be like a suitcase so crammed full you'd never be able to close the lid. Or like an ice cream so huge that the cornet would be far too tiny to support it, and you'd need at least a dozen flakes. Maybe more.

'I'm going to ask her out.'

I said it before I could stop myself. I slammed my big mouth shut but the words had already leapt out into the open.

Matty only shrugged at me. He was probably thinking that I didn't stand a chance. He was probably thinking that Hannah was way out of my league, that she wouldn't look at me twice, would not even remember my name. And I was suddenly embarrassed, completely blushing up. I instantly regretted saying anything, especially in front of Matty, and hurried away to find my packed lunch and then the dining hall.

I thought about Hannah all dinner long as I slowly munched on my sandwiches. She was special. She was probably the only thing the whole of our year agreed on (or at least the lads anyway). Some of us would argue that OJ Simpson was indeed innocent, a few would maybe claim that UFOs existed, and maybe even a couple of the kids in Mr Mooder's class still believed the earth was flat. But ask any of us who was the best looking girl ever to set foot inside the comp and you'd hear the same name repeated over and over again: Hannah Olivia Parks. You could lay good money on it. I doubt many of us would even hesitate; there'd certainly be no need for multiple choice. Cut and dried; Hannah was the most beautiful girl any of us had ever met. She'd only been at the comp for a couple of terms back in year eight, but we'd all enjoyed many pleasurable nights dreaming about her, then suffered many miserable mornings back in the real world. I knew the news of her return would send shock waves throughout the year. I could see them all sitting around me now, daydreaming zombies with mushed-up half-eaten cottage pie and carrot on their plates, and spilled gravy on their chins. And I cursed Matty for having such a loose tongue. He was meant to be my friend, he shouldn't have told anybody else, just me, not them.

But the news was everywhere, and for once Chinese whispers was a lie, because this piece of intelligence was far too important to distort. I saw Ali, Dave and Jase huddled whispering about it in the cloakroom. Then saw Jase, Kev and Nicko in the library. Then Nicko, Mark and the two Steves in the queue for the tuck shop. Then the two Steves, Ali and Dave back in the cloakroom again. Robbie Baxter asked me in history if I'd heard, he seemed very excited. And Becky Flowers had suddenly become the (second) most popular girl in school. Swarms of year ten lads followed her up and down the corridors, hung around waiting for her at the end of lessons or outside the girls' toilets, all wanting to know if it was true. Was Hannah really coming back for the summer? But Becky had never been one for attention and was soon swinging her bag in faces and stamping her boots on toes.

Matty loved it all, obviously. He was the hero of the piece. He'd been the first to know, so when Becky and the other girls kept their mouths firmly shut everybody rushed to Matty to hear once again how he'd discovered the most prodigious news of the year. Because unlike Becky he had no qualms about telling his story. But then again, he had no qualms about telling anybody anything really.

He had a crowd around him at the end of the day. There was a bunch of maybe as many as a dozen lads all talking to him at once as he walked to the bike sheds. I lagged a little way behind. Matty and I always cycled home together so I thought I had plenty of time to pump him for information, but he obviously didn't want to leave the company of his entourage today and walked with them instead, pushing his bike along.

He was a pale, forgettable kid, with cheap trainers and hair that desperately wanted to be combed, if only it knew which way. He was usually uncool enough to have to spend break time on his own. Or with me. The only difference between us was that I didn't mind all that much about being the last to be picked for a team during games (as long as I got to play) or that I was often overlooked by the year's requisite 'in crowd' and their parties (which were generally embarrassing farces anyway — everyone knew parties didn't get any good until you hit the sixth form and at least looked old enough to buy beer). Leave me alone with my guitar and Paul Weller's latest and I'd be more than happy. But Matty saw his lack of chic as a curse. As long as I'd known him it had been an endeavour of his to reach the comp's 'A' list. He aspired to classroom credibility.

I was still following a little way behind his new-found followers with my own bike when he spotted me. He had their full attention for the time being but must have been running short of different ways to tell the same story. He needed a new angle. He stopped on the corner of

Carvard Avenue and the group around him stopped too, hanging on his every word. He betrayed me with little more than a second's hesitation.

'Andy reckons he's going to ask her out.' It was said as an accusation and he even pointed a finger at me when he said it, condemning me.

I suppose I should have protested innocence, but that would have been like betraying Hannah wouldn't it? And I didn't really have the time to anyway.

The outrage erupted from the group of boys in colourful language. It was an instant burst of anger as the dozen or so boys all turned on me. I was scared some of them might even come for me, but fortunately it quickly settled into a steady torrent of abuse and name-calling and I managed to shrug most of it off. But the look on Matty's face bit deep. He was supposed to be my friend. He comforted the others by telling them that I didn't stand a chance, that Hannah would certainly laugh in my face. I wished I'd had the courage to stand and defend myself, but all I wanted to do was get on my bike and ride away. Which I did, heading straight home, knowing that my school status had suddenly shifted from dull, inconsequential kid at the back who hands his homework in on time, to hazard, threat, ENEMY.

Keith Gray

I realised the following day at school was going to be
difficult and worried about it for most of the night, fearing
the worst. Then those very fears came true the next
morning when Carl Peterson cornered me in the toilets
before chemistry. I saw him come in and zipped myself
up quickly, just in case. He blocked my way to the sink to
wash my hands.

He didn't mention her name, there was no need. 'Matty
said you're gonna ask her out. Maybe she won't wanna go
out with a sap like you? What d'you think about that?'
He was bigger than me. Not just taller but wider too. He
was in the comp's rugby team and played every chance
he got, on and off the field.

I shrugged.

He'd broken his nose in a game against Stonner
Secondary School but had refused to leave the match
before the final whistle. It was now crushed into his square
face and reminded me of a fat question mark. His spotty
face looked red, angry, inflamed. 'Maybe I wanna ask her
out. What d'you think about that?'

I shrugged again.

He took a step towards me, forcing me to take a step
away from him. 'I'll fight you for her. What d'you think
about that? You and me. The winner gets to ask her out.'

He interpreted my third shrug in a row as a Yes. 'Friday, after school.' He laughed at me. 'Sap.' And pushed me another step away from him with a sharp, painful jab in my shoulder. But then left me alone to contemplate my future, which somehow felt as if it had suddenly shrunk, like a woolly jumper in the boil wash.

I leaned on the cold, white basin and stared at myself in the smeared mirror. The question Peterson's nose had posed wasn't whether to fight him for the right to ask Hannah out or not, I knew I'd do that no matter what. The question was, would she want to spend the summer with me if I won? I had spots too, you see. Not as bad as Peterson's admittedly, but bad (and noticeable) enough. I had a strange face, stretched and oval, and too many teeth for my mouth. I wasn't pretty, though I guessed I was prettier than Peterson. What would someone as truly beautiful as Hannah see in me?

But I remembered sitting next to her in geography for the short time she'd been here, one of the envied few who'd shared a lesson with her. We'd spent quite a lot of time talking together, and not just about where to find the Andes either. I knew she had a kitten called Louis who'd turned out to be a girl and so had had to be renamed Louise. I also knew that she wanted to go away to university and train to be a journalist, and one day wanted to live in a big house by the sea. She knew quite a lot about me too come to think of it, about my dreams of musical stardom. And she'd always laughed at my impressions of the teacher, Mr Minnett, even though they weren't very good really. So maybe I did stand a chance. I offered myself a considered look. Yes, maybe I did. And the look turned to one of set determination.

Which was the look I managed to keep for almost the whole of chemistry. I would maybe have been able to make it all the way through to the end of the lesson if it hadn't been for the two Steves. I was in the middle of clearing away my books and wondering where would be the safest place to hide during break when they sidled over to me. I pretended to be pleased to see them but knew they'd been among Matty's new-found disciples the day before.

Steve One sat himself down on my left. He was the good-looking one; dark hair, deep-set eyes and already growing a moustache (not because it suited him, simply because he could). 'Is it true you and Peterson are having a fight?'

Steve Two stood to my left. His hair was long and greasy and his front teeth were broken from when he'd fallen off the swings as a kid. He had one green eye and one kind of blue. Like David Bowie, or the stray mongrel my auntie once found. 'It's a duel over Hannah, isn't it?'

I have to admit that I quite liked the idea of thinking of the fight as a duel, it added to the romance I was building in my head, so I told them that yes it was indeed true.

Steve One scoffed, a kind of snorted laugh. 'He'll kill you.'

'You're dead meat.' Steve Two echoed his friend's scorn.

I decided not to tell the first Steve he was trailing the cuff of his shirt in the puddle of hydrochloric acid I'd spilled earlier, and I refused to look the second one in his mismatched eyes. But then they both surprised me even further.

'I'm going to take the winner on.'

'And me.'

I think the shock showed on my face.

'We don't think it's fair that only you and Peterson get the chance to ask her out.'

'Anybody should be able to ask her out.'

'Anybody.'

'Yeah.'

And apparently they weren't the only ones to feel this way because by the end of the morning's lessons Robbie

Baxter, Alan Dickson, Jase and Tom Block were all limbering up ready to fight me for the chance to ask Hannah to spend the summer with them. The word was spreading and more and more people were coming up to me and telling me they wanted to beat me to a pulp. By the time the last lesson of the day rolled around the list was twenty names long. Even Matty appeared on it, which I have to admit was particularly galling. I would have told him so too on the way home, but he was busy with his new friends.

I wasn't sure how to feel about all of these people wanting to fight with me. I wasn't sure whether it made my chances any better or simply a lot worse. Maybe all the big kids like Peterson could be knocked out or exhausted by the time they got their turn to have a go at me. And I was still surprised by just how many were willing to try their luck against these big kids. But then I remembered exactly what the prize was at stake here: one summer with Hannah. I realised I couldn't blame them.

I supposed we should all think ourselves lucky that Jez Cartwright hadn't decided to put his name down, and we could only hope he never did. If Peterson was big, Jez Cartwright was bigger, the comp's resident hulk. Jez Cartwright was a gorilla, in looks as well as stature. As I cycled to school on that Wednesday morning I prayed he wouldn't get wind of what was happening and fancy a bit of the action too. Even *my* commitment might waver if he did.

I was half expecting him to approach me when I got to school and scurried to my form room as quickly as I could. Luckily he was nowhere to be seen (was in fact probably twagging it again), but Paul Stewart did grab me as soon as I set foot inside the room. I hadn't even had time to drop my bag on to my desk when he threw a fake-friendly arm around my shoulder and flipped open a little black notebook he was carrying.

'Care to put a small wager on your chances in the big fight, Andy?' He flicked his long, blond fringe from out of his eyes and winked at me. He was possibly the best looking lad in the year, or at least was the one whose name was written on most of the girl's pencil cases. He'd probably never seen a tube of Oxy in his life, his skin was absolutely blemish-free, and his teeth fitted into his smile perfectly. He looked like a pop star. And knew it.

I scanned down the page of the notebook. The list had grown by another ten names or so (still no Jez Cartwright I was pleased to see). Then I looked down the column of odds Paul had written beside them. Peterson

was the favourite, closely followed by Steve Number Two.
I was the rank outsider at 100 to 1. Even Matty was only
30 to 1!

'Get stuffed, Stewart.' I nastily shrugged his arm from
round my shoulder. The other boys in the classroom started
laughing, egging him on.

'Now don't be like that. Chris has put ten pence on
you, haven't you Chris?' And his stupid lapdog of a friend
gave me the thumbs-up. 'See? He's got faith in you, Andy,
lad.'

I wanted to storm out, maybe should have, right there
and then, but first I dug in my trouser pocket for my dinner
money and virtually threw the pound coin at him. 'You
better have that hundred quid ready on Friday.' Then I
stormed out, ignoring the jeers and catcalls that hassled
me all the way to the door.

'Just don't wuss out on us.' Paul Stewart followed me
into the corridor. 'All bets are forfeit if you don't turn up.'

I ignored him.

I couldn't go into dinner that day and spent it alone
in the library. I was sick and tired of people coming up to
me, feeling my biceps and tutting loudly or asking me if
I liked hospital food. I saw Matty hanging around the
tuck shop with Paul Stewart and Chris Ganin but didn't

go to talk to him. I just hoped he was happy with his new friends.

The fight was set for Friday, the last day of term, as soon as school kicked out. We all had to make our way to the park at the bottom of Wollston Hill and there a massive square would be marked out in the grass. Everybody would fight together (all thirty-eight of us), the idea being to force each other out of the square's boundaries. The last one still in the ring would be the winner and would get to ask Hannah out. It was a fight to the finish, no time limit, and the only rule being no weapons other than fists or feet allowed. Paul Stewart had been going to referee, but now reckoned he fancied his chances as well (he'd put himself down as second favourite in fact) so one of the sixth-formers had been bribed to do it instead.

Wednesday night was a sleepless one for me, and not because of thoughts of Hannah either. When I got to school on Thursday morning I found a box of plasters and a roll of bandages on my desk. Matty usually sat next to me during registration but had now moved his chair to sit next to the two Steves. Carl Peterson pushed his rugby-crushed nose into my face and offered to beat me up that afternoon instead. 'Then you don't need to turn up tomorrow. What d'you think about that?' And Paul

Stewart told me my odds had lengthened to 150 to 1, but in the unlikely event that I did win he'd still only have to pay me one hundred pounds because they were the odds when I'd placed my bet. 'Sorry.'

But by Friday morning things had suddenly changed, and a lot of people had suddenly lost their appetite for the fight. The word flying around the classrooms and the boys' toilets that morning was that Jez Cartwright's name had suddenly appeared in Paul Stewart's little black notebook, and a lot of people weren't too willing to fight with a living ape-man. Not that they admitted it. Although I've got to confess that the quicker home time rushed towards me, the closer I also came to chickening out. I could have easily done it too. All I really had to do was let one of the girls know what we were planning and then it was sure to fall through. We'd kept it a secret from them this far because even we weren't stupid enough to think Hannah would be flattered by what we were planning; not in the nineties, not with all of the political correctness and stuff we get drummed into us nowadays. I knew that if I accidentally let mention of it slip to Nicky Hudson say, or even Becky Flowers, well . . .

I didn't though. I *had* to fight. But no longer simply because of Hannah.

The final lesson of the year was a nightmare. It was English and I had Paul Stewart and the two Steves in my class. Not to mention Matty who I had to sit next to. He kept winking at the others and wrote DEAD on the knuckles of his right hand and MEAT on the knuckles of his left. Which made him look pretty silly when he put his fists together on top of his desk and he realised what he'd done, but it still wound my stomach that little bit tighter. It was so hot in that classroom. The sun blazed away outside and there were thunder clouds growing in the stifling afternoon air as well as inside my belly.

By the time we were all finally let out it had started to rain. I didn't care. I imagined pushing certain people's faces into the squelchy mud. I also had a plan for just such an occurrence anyway. I lived only a street or so over from the park and hurried home to put my football boots on. These would give me extra grip on the wet grass, as well as an added toe-stomping, calf-kicking advantage. The sky cracked and rumbled around me as I ran through the streets, the rain coming down in buckets.

It could have only taken me ten minutes tops to fetch my boots and get back to the park again, but when I arrived I thought I must have missed everything. I cursed myself; surely I wasn't too late? The only person standing around in the pouring rain was Matty, his shoulders hunched against the heavy drops and his lank fringe plastered to his forehead. I thought he was maybe here to gloat at me missing the fight. I walked over to where he was standing by the duck pond and braced myself for the humiliation that was to come.

But he looked less than pleased to see me. 'Oh. Yeah. Er, hi.' He looked around himself nervously. 'Seen anybody else on your way, like?'

'Hasn't anybody else turned up?'

He shook his head slowly, not looking quite so brave without his new friends to wink at. The rain swept over him in sheets. 'Must be the weather.'

'Just you and me is it?' I couldn't believe all these *big hard men* had bailed out because of the rain. Or maybe it was because of the threat of Jez Cartwright. And I began to wonder if the big kid's name ever had actually appeared on the list anyway, or if Paul Stewart had simply been hedging his bets.

Matty made one final attempt to demean me. 'Lucky for you they're not here, like. Must be your birthday or something.' But we both knew it didn't work. 'Not that I ever wanted you to get hurt anyway.' He tried a different tack. 'We've always been friends, like.'

He noticed me looking at the graffiti on his knuckles and hastily shoved his hands in his pockets. He took a step away from me. He shrugged his sodden and sagging shoulders and tried to flick his fringe from out of his eyes without taking his incriminating hands from out of his pockets. He looked very wet, very lost, very uncomfortable. I almost felt sorry for him. Almost. We stood facing each other down, the torrential rain howling around us. Streaks of lightning flashed and crackled above our heads.

He offered me an awkward, half-drowned smile. Then took another step backwards. 'Better give them five minutes, yeah?'

I nodded. I gave them ten. Then kicked him in the goolies and pushed him backwards into the duck pond. Well, he was already wet anyway.

I did end up having a pretty good summer that year (admittedly maybe only ten flakes in my ice cream instead of the full twelve), but spent it without Hannah. I bumped into her a couple of times wandering around town with Becky Flowers and some of the other girls. I didn't say much to her, just pulled off my Mr Minnett impersonation on request and enquired after Louis(e). She was still incredibly beautiful, still the most wonderful girl to ever set foot inside the comp. But she told me she may be back next summer, so maybe I'll try my luck then. And after all, if I save the money Paul Stewart owes me I'll be at least one hundred pounds better off, and will be able to take her somewhere really posh.

The Real Song

Annie Dalton

I went to see Zak Tyler today. When I got home I crawled into bed, planning to howl myself to sleep. But I must have cried myself out on the train. No matter how much I bashed my pillow, my troubles went on blazing inside my head, like a hundred watt bulb I couldn't switch off.

It's almost four thirty now and I've given up. I'm lying on my bedroom rug, with the stereo down low, wearing Zak's sweater and listening to the track that was my secret theme tune for us. And I'm praying for a sign, something, anything to help me get through this and out the other side.

My parents keep insisting they know what's best for me. But they're so, so wrong. I didn't let myself down by getting mixed up with Zak, to quote Mum's words. And I wasn't throwing all their kindness back in their faces, to quote my dad.

Zak's got nothing to do with them and everything to do with me.

They say they don't know me any more. The truth is, they never did.

Our family has lived in Oxford since I can remember. We moved to this house in Jericho when my mum landed a contract with the BBC. My parents are so successful, it's scary. My dad's Irish-Italian and Mum grew up in Milk River, Jamaica. Mum doesn't look black, unless you know what you're looking for. She's lighter skinned than either Tosh or me and because of that people gave her a hard time when she was small. White nigger, people called her. White cockroach.

Probably that's why Mum divorced Jamaica the day she stepped on to the tarmac at Heathrow. She wouldn't even go over for the funeral when my grandma died. As Mum says, she's come a long way. No one calls us names in Oxford. Instead they invite us to every party going.

The beautiful, talented, interracial Rossettis.

Did you know there's a kind of politeness that makes you want to scream so hard you can feel the fishbone burn of it deep in your throat from just imagining it? Well some days that's how I feel, knowing I've got to walk into another room full of polite smiling people.

'So this is Alice. What a beauty. Wouldn't you kill for that *marvellous* pre-Raphaelite hair.'

Once when Tosh was small and some horrible woman went raving on about his big brown eyes, he said sweetly, 'Yes, but don't you think it's such a shame I've got to grow up?'

The wrong kind of admiration is like radioactive fallout, leaching calcium from your bones, poisoning you with other people's unreality. Until you long to slip out of the prison of your skin for just one minute, and say, 'Hey, it's me in here, you know.'

Only by the time I was twelve, I wasn't sure there was anyone inside my skin any more. Maybe pretty was all I was. Pretty and empty.

Every time one of my school-friends said, 'Alice, you're so drop dead gorgeous, you should be a model,' I felt a little colder, a little emptier. By the age of sixteen I had several cubic feet of freezer space inside me where beautiful

Annie Dalton

Alice Rossetti was meant to be.

It didn't help that Mum and Dad never acted proud of anything about me except the storm-tossed princess looks I inherited from them.

Mum and Dad first met when they were students, working for some peace group. But at some point, while they were working day and night to afford a smarter house, a newer dishwasher, school fees – the peace idea must have got lost. Because, whatever peace looks like, it can't look remotely like Sunday lunch at our house.

The summer I met Zak, my parents were their furthest ever from peace in our time. Their crockery-hurling phase was stressful, but the year-long silence that followed was deadly.

Then one night Tosh said, 'Dad's got someone else.'

And I said, 'I know.'

And we went back to watching *Breakfast at Tiffany's*. That weepy bit where she finds her cat in the rain.

Since my GCSEs finished, I'd caught the habit of watching old Audrey Hepburn movies through the night, until the sky grew light enough to risk closing my eyes. Sometimes Tosh drifted in too, draped in his bedspread, and watched with me, till he crashed out on my floor.

Then next morning, I'd turn my stereo back on,

wishing Kate hadn't deserted me for the summer to do her posh cooking course. I knew what she'd say, though. 'When things get this bad, Alice, you need a sign.' Kate's a great one for signs and wonders.

So when I saw Larry's ad in the window of The Red Rock Cafe, I hoped this was it. My sign.

The cafe door was wedged open, leaking coffee fumes. At the back was a summery courtyard, a rampant vine. And then I recognised it. Even through the din of the Cowley road, the bass line pounded through the soles of my feet, up my spine and into my skull. The exact hiphop track I'd been playing all summer. Even I can't miss a sign like that.

I didn't give myself time to think, just shook my hair back, undid my shirt one button lower than Mum likes, strode in, right on the beat, asked Larry for the job and got it, all before the track finished. Meanwhile the other Red Rock girls were whizzing about in their micro-minis like waitress supermodels.

I felt as smug as if I'd auditioned for RADA. For the first time in months I had something to wake up for.

The other girls were great too, once you knew them; specially Lottie. And I'd never met anyone like Larry's manager. Travis ran the cafe the days Larry was busy with our London branch and looked exactly like an angel in an Italian painting. He had the sweetest smile I ever saw on an adult. He was a sweet person too and always took the trouble to make everyone feel special, even customers who made me break into a rash of irritation.

Some nights we'd go back to his place, a legal squat he shared with some girls over an Indian restaurant. We'd take the cassette player and a bottle of wine up on to the roof. I could have stayed up there for ever, gazing over the city in the dark.

Once a police helicopter hovered above us for hours, its searchlights strobing down. I felt as if I was starring in a film about young people in a city.

'Watch out, Travis,' someone said, 'they're on to you, mate,' and we all laughed.

That was the night I fell asleep under the stars and didn't get home till five in the morning.

Tosh was still up, lying on my rug watching *Roman Holiday*. He didn't even turn his head when I came in, just shrugged himself deeper inside his smelly dressing gown and said, 'If you're having sex with Travis, Alice, I hope it's the safe kind.' But his voice was gritty with worry.

'Idiot,' I said. 'No one has sex with Travis. It would be like doing it with the Angel Gabriel.'

But secretly I wished that instead of staying on for A levels, I could leave home and join that irresistible party that sprang up wherever Travis turned his archangel's smile.

The night Zak Tyler strolled in off the street, I was serving some American tourists and set their garlic bread down so much harder than I meant to their candle blew out.

It had been a long hot day and Zak was wearing flawless jeans and a leather waistcoat without a stitch under it. The closest I can get to describing the colour of his skin is amber because amber is full of light and so was he. His hair was cropped close except for a lightning flash where a white person's parting would be. And his eyes were almost as shy as mine.

It was so warm you could smell the whole city blowing in through the door; petrochemicals, honeysuckle, coffee beans and bad drains. And with a terrifying rush, as if I'd returned from a far distant galaxy, I woke up back inside my own life.

Zak ordered a beer. Travis cracked a joke. His entire face kind of dazzled with humour. Then it was like films when the soundtrack switches back on and I realised Larry had asked me three times for more ice.

When I came out, Zak was waiting, holding a rose

he'd stolen from one of our tables. He handed it over and said, 'Travis says he's never got anywhere with you, but that you know everything worth knowing about hip-hop. So can I walk you back?'

I hate to say this, but I used to feel uneasy around black guys; those smooth-talking brothers, with their high octane flirting. But it didn't matter with Zak that I couldn't speak *patois* even if I was on fire. Somehow there we still were, wheeling my bike across Magdalen Bridge, as if we'd known each other our whole lives.

'I'd buy you a drink,' he said later, as we walked down Little Clarendon Street, 'but I've only got these.' Rather surprisingly he showed me a handful of ludo counters.

'Jade's always raiding my pockets,' he said. 'Jade's my daughter,' he explained. 'But – er, Carmen, her mother, ain't in the picture now. Okay, Alice?'

'Okay,' I echoed, dazed. 'How – how old is –?'

'Jade? Nineteen months,' said Zak. 'She can say twelve words. My own old man shoved off, as it goes. I won't ever do that to Jade.'

'No,' I said. Zak's eyes were too bright to look at. I could see all of him at once. The hurt and the sweetness.

'I like things straight. No being economical with the truth, if you get me. My life's not a nice life, Alice. But

I'm not ashamed,' he added softly. 'It's just my life. Understand?'

And he leaned across my bike, kissing me so confidently that for the next twenty-four hours, I had violent, delicious flashbacks. And that's how we began.

'Does he sell drugs?' Tosh asked me.

'What, because he's young, black and male he must be a drug dealer?'

'Keep your hair on, Rossetti. You said he dropped out of school when he was my age,' said Tosh. 'You said he doesn't believe in claiming the dole. It was also you who said he's got a baby daughter to support. *You* tell me what his career options are.'

'The same as yours, if you spend your whole life indoors playing on computers,' I said cruelly.

'So he does sell drugs.'

'Tosh, drop it. He hates hard drugs, if that's what worries you. He sells weed that's all. Mostly he works for a friend who runs a decorating business and his sister minds Jade.'

'Okay,' said Tosh, patting my hand. 'I just don't want *my* sister hurt. Now hush, it's the best bit.'

So we watched Tosh's favourite scene in *Sabrina Fair*,

where Humphrey Bogart punches his brother's lights out, because they're both in love with Audrey Hepburn.

Zak was intrigued by Tosh too. 'So what's this story about the police?' he asked, as we helped Jade feed the ducks in Magdalen College Gardens.

I told him about the night Tosh reported an abandoned car.

'Some idiots crashed outside our house, and jumped out leaving the engine running. The police told Tosh to wait beside it. He was wetting himself, convinced it was going to explode, like in films. Then the cops arrived and accused *him* of stealing it! They wouldn't believe he lived in our house. So he showed them his door key. They said, 'How do we know you haven't stolen that, you little creep.' He didn't have a clue where Mum and Dad were. And our neighbours said, maybe Tosh had done it. They weren't sure. The police were going to arrest him, Zak! Then I turned up and started screaming that Tosh was my brother and had been for fourteen years. And they went away.'

Zak's impassive expression didn't flicker. 'He was stupid to phone them,' he said calmly. 'Still, he knows better now.'

'That's a terrible thing to say.'

'And it's reality,' he said. 'And if Tosh want to stay sane he got to *know* that.'

Jade trundled up in her ankle-length frock and a pair of joke sunglasses, to show her daddy a ring-pull she'd found. 'Money money,' she chanted in her husky little voice. 'Look, money money money.'

'Bwoy, Jade,' said Zak, gently taking it from her. 'You find any more of this Martian currency and we'll show Alice a kicking time in some neighbouring galaxy, eh?'

'Tosh mostly stays indoors now,' I went on. 'I think he feels if he goes out, he's too . . .' I searched for the word. 'Too *visible*. Like an accident, that's just waiting to happen.'

Zak adjusted Jade's sun hat. 'But that can't work,' he said grimly. 'He's acting like *he's* the one who's got to be ashamed. A man's got to respect himself and teach people to respect him back. Your brother needs straightening out. Man to man.' Then he looked up and saw my face. 'What? What's wrong?'

'Nothing,' I said, swallowing. 'It's just – we never talk about this stuff at home. When things like . . . like that happen, I go numb. Act like it's all some far-off movie happening to someone else. But since I met you, I've started to feel so much. I feel everything. And I'm – scared.' The word caught in my throat.

He kissed me then, small kisses from my bare shoulder to my cheek and Jade joined in, crooning tenderly, 'Oh no cry, no cry, sweet'art.'

I pulled away, crying seriously now, but he held on fiercely. 'But I want you to feel, Alice, when you're with me,' he whispered into my hair.

Then he said, 'Travis just went to London for the weekend. He said we could use his place.'

And suddenly I was laughing through my tears like a crazy girl, saying, 'Oh God, Zak, it had better be safe sex then, or Tosh will give me hell.'

Zak and I did borrow Travis's attic room that night.

But we didn't have sex in his antique iron bed, safe or otherwise.

When it came to it, I was too scared. Oh, not that Zak would hurt me or that the stupid condom would break and I'd get a disease, or get pregnant, like Carmen. It wasn't even because Travis's flatmates were watching an ancient horror video downstairs, knowing perfectly well why we were there.

It was what I told Zak by the river. He made me feel too much.

When he took me in his arms, this drowning terror

seized me and I started shaking. Once I started, I couldn't stop.

I thought he'd hate me. But he was lovely.

'Sweetheart, it really ain't no big deal. We got our whole lives. So what we'll do, we'll cuddle up and when you feel a bit better, we'll just drift off to sleep.'

And to the familiar soundtrack of a police helicopter hovering over East Oxford, Zak stroked my hair over and over, murmuring softly, until, at last, I stopped shivering.

I was almost asleep, my limbs warm and floating when I sensed him smiling beside me in the dark. 'You know this old bed, Alice,' he said dreamily. 'It exactly like the one my mother born in, back in Milk River.'

I turned to him amazed. 'Did you say Milk River?'

'Mmn.'

'That's where my mum comes from. That must be why it feels so . . . familiar, listening to you. Mum keeps her Milk River voice under armed guard these days,' I explained. 'But when we were small, it still broke out from time to time.'

'When she vex, eh,' said Zak amused.

But the good soft floating feeling was gone now. I sat up, my shoulders stiff with remembering how much I had loved Mum's Jamaican voice warming me inside, like ginger tea. Her whole body seeming to dance to music only she could hear.

How long had it been, since she hugged me and meant it? How long since she looked at me, and really saw me? Was it possible she didn't notice Tosh turning into a politely panicking ghost of himself, or had she just lived in this cold country so long, she plain didn't care?

'Lately I can't even remember how Mum sounds. Do you know what I do sometimes? Promise you won't laugh. I play her answerphone message. 'Sorry we can't take your call just now . . .'

Zak reached out, wordlessly touching my cheek.

Searchlights flickered over our bed. The helicopter was returning, its blades churning up the night.

'I've been alone,' I said, my throat closing with grief. 'I've been alone so long.'

'Yeah,' said Zak softly, pulling me close. 'Yeah, little sister, you have. But now at last you find your way home.'

'You mean I'm finally going to meet him?' said Tosh.

'When he fetches Jade,' I said. 'And, Tosh, Zak always looks incredibly smart. So you might think about finding a T-shirt that hasn't got quite so much ketchup on it.'

Tosh anxiously checked his reflection. 'Tell the truth.

My hair doesn't look too cool, does it.'

'Not exactly cool,' I said carefully. 'Zak could cut it for you. He does his friends' hair.'

'Yeah? Could he do a fade? Could he do, like a flash, just here?'

'Maybe you should stick with a straight fade,' I told him. 'Or Mum will kill you.'

'So why are we babysitting Jade, again?'

I lifted Zak's daughter up, hooking her sturdy little legs over my hip, as though I'd been carrying babies all my life. 'Because Zak's working and his sister's not well.'

'Drug dealer working or decorator working?'

'Tosh, we exhausted that conversation weeks ago.'

'So it's drug dealing then.'

It was Lottie who phoned me, after the police raided the Red Rock and arrested Zak and Travis.

I'm such a fool. I really hadn't guessed about the sideline Travis was running, all those days Larry was away.

I suppose the cafe offered the perfect border post, positioned between respectable Magdalen Bridge and wicked Blackbird Leys. And I can remember vividly now, though I didn't notice them at the time, Travis's special customers who drifted casually round the back 'for a chat'.

But Zak didn't lie to me. Because though they found this huge stash of crack cocaine in Larry's kitchen, all they found on Zak was a small quantity of weed. The trouble was, when Zak was Tosh's age, he got caught stealing a car stereo. So the weed was enough to send him to jail.

Young Offenders, to be accurate. Zak isn't quite nineteen.

First they searched me, then I followed everyone into a hideous hall, which reminded me of exams. It's only months since I took my GCSEs, but it might as well have been a thousand years. I sat at the bare little table, my mouth dry with nerves. An officer unlocked a second door and they filed through; the dangerous animals being unleashed into the circus tent.

When Zak came in, with his loose street-wary walk, my insides gave a lurch. He was the same. Changed, sad, but the same. Even in prison denims, he was full of light, his eyes still almost as shy as mine.

'You're letting your hair grow,' I said.

He bumped my cheekbone when we kissed. I was shaking.

'This is a lousy place you picked for our date,' he joked,

trying to lighten things. 'Bet no one's even taken your order.'

Later he said, 'The only reason I'm letting go of your hand is I don't want them bastards to think you're passing me something.'

'They're not looking,' I said.

'Oh, they're looking,' he said bitterly. 'Believe me.' He avoided my eyes as if being in prison had taught him things he was ashamed to know.

'Think that coffee machine would take Martian currency?' I asked, to bring him back. 'I spent all my earth money getting here.'

Zak broke into a sad little smile. 'I can't believe you remembered that.'

'I remember everything,' I said, stroking his ice-cold hand. 'You used to be so warm.'

'So did you,' he said, so fiercely I blushed.

You can't say the things you want to there, with the officers staring dead ahead with regulation switched-off expressions, radios crackling. The real talk was in our eyes.

Zak kept twisting his new dreads. You could see he didn't know he was doing it.

Half a dozen or so little kids were dashing up and down.

'How's Jade?' I said, watching them.

'The social worker says she's settling.' Zak ran his hand over his face. Another new gesture. 'It's hard to be happy for her, when "settling" means forgetting me.'

'Couldn't Carmen have her? She is her mother.'

Zak's face clouded. 'Only thing Carmen care about is partying. She shouldn't ever have had a kid.'

'You liked her once. It took two of you, you know, to make Jade.'

'I know how many it took,' said Zak angrily. Then he checked himself, flashing a wicked grin. 'Shame it wasn't you, eh? You look good enough to stop traffic. And you smell so sweet. I was lying awake one night, trying to think what you smell like, and it's fresh clean ironing.'

'Ironing!' I said, so offended Zak laughed out loud, husky peals of beautiful, uncontrollable laughter. Then just as abruptly he stopped, running his hands over his face again, grinding in his knuckles. They came away wet.

'I don't know how this happened, Alice,' he said. 'How did it happen?'

Afterwards, outside the gates, an elderly black woman wept, her voice rising and falling like a song. 'So many,' she kept saying. 'So many beautiful black boys in jail.'

I could hear her, all the way back to Oxford.

It's almost morning. Almost a new day and I can still hear her. And behind the painsoaked rhythms of her voice, other voices, whose names are lost, but whose sufferings will be part of me for ever and whose strength is also mine.

So many. So many.

And slowly, gently, without drum rolls or even an accelerated heartbeat, it dawns on me that this is the sign I prayed for.

I've come home at last. And I know what I'm going to do.

I'm going back to school. So I can make a difference.

Years ago, my mother dreamt of peace. But Zak taught me you can't have peace in this world until you know which reality you're dealing with. Until you know who you are. And now that I know, if I don't fight to make things better, then I'm just another piece of the problem, aren't I?

Listen. Last summer I bought a hip-hop album. The moment I played it, I was hooked. This music knows me better than I know myself, expressing feelings I never even knew I had. The fit is so tight, it could have been designed as my own personal soundtrack. But there's one track I think of as the *real* song. The song I've been singing inside my heart all my life without knowing it.

And that's how it was with Zak. Even before I met him, he was the song inside my heart. In the loneliest craziest summer of my life, Zak Tyler was the one real song. That's what he was.